What Once Was Broken

S.L. STERLING

Editor: Brandi Aquino, Editing Done Write
Cover Design: Thunderstruck Cover Design

ABOUT THE BOOK

Darling Ranch. It was a family name in this town, a family business and a family way of life.

Over the past year, the place hadn't felt like family, or home, and I was barely staying in business.

My wife had died from an aneurism while pregnant with our first child. It happened one morning while I was out in the field tending to the animals. The doctors told me it wouldn't have mattered had I of been by her side, the outcome would have been the same. Still, I beat myself up.

My best friend and neighbor, Gabe Bentley knew this. He let me mourn my own way, but now he's pushing me harder than ever.

"What's the rush?" I asked him one morning.

"I'm being deployed. I need to know my sister and the farm are taken care of....by the only man I trust in this town...you."

I'd known the army was recruiting again but I didn't know he'd been called upon. I also didn't know Cadence was back in town. I really didn't know if I could be the man, the friend, the rancher that he needed me to be.

What I did know?

No matter how much it pained me, I'd try to do whatever it took to make sure that I didn't let Gabe down.

Then I saw Cadence and for the first time since my wife

died I actually thought I could heal. She made me feel alive, made the pain go away. So why did I feel so guilty? One minute I was longing to hold her, the next I was pushing her away, until I finally pushed too hard and sent her running.

I didn't want to fail my best friend, and I didn't want to fail Cadence. We all needed our Christmas wish and I decided to do whatever it took to make sure we got it.

Connor

August 2022

I wiped my eyes, blinked a few times, and looked at the clock. It was just before three and still dark outside. I sat up on the edge of the bed and stretched. I had to get down to the barn to check on the recent additions I'd added to the cattle barn from Jenkins ranch, plus I had two cattle ready to give birth anytime. It was going to be busy for the next few days.

The mattress creaked as I shifted my weight. I stilled, careful not to wake Ella, who was sleeping soundly. She was almost eight months pregnant and hadn't been feeling well for the past few days. She needed her rest, the last thing I wanted to do was wake her. I leaned over and reached for my jeans on the bedside table, and sure enough, that was when I felt the bed shift.

I froze at the sound of her moan, hoping that I hadn't woken her. I paused, almost afraid to breathe, as I waited to see if she was awake. Another small moan, and then I felt her hand on my arm. "Connor? What's wrong? What time is it? Where are you going?"

"It's early, baby, really early. Go back to sleep. It's not time for you to get up yet," I whispered, taking her small hand in mine.

"No, it's okay. I'll get up and get you breakfast before you head out," she murmured, pushing the covers off her, trying to sit up.

I softly smiled as I slipped into my jeans. "It's okay, Ella. It's nowhere near time to eat. Now, sweetie, go back to sleep and get some rest so you can finish growing that baby. Now, I've got to go move the cattle to the field and get the new cattle fed, then check on the two that are due." Pressing a kiss to her forehead, I pulled the covers up over her again. "I'll be a bit."

"Okay. I'll have breakfast ready at six when you come in."

"Sounds good." I pressed a kiss to her lips.

I slipped into the small washroom off our room and quickly splashed some water on my face, thinking back to earlier this past month. Ella hadn't been feeling well. She couldn't pinpoint the problem, and that had me worried. The doctor assured us everything was fine and ordered her to get some extra rest until the baby was born, but Ella was stubborn. Since he'd told her to take it easy, she'd done the exact opposite.

Deep down I knew she'd been doing too much, so I'd tried to help her around the house, but she wouldn't hear of it. It surprised me she'd listened to me just now and had gone back to sleep. That alone told me she was exhausted, normally she'd have gotten up regardless of what I said.

I came out of the washroom to check on her before heading down to the fields to find she was sound asleep again. I grabbed my jacket off the end of the bed and made my way downstairs and out into the darkness.

As I finished moving the last of the cattle to the field, I drove back up to the barn and hopped off the quad in time to see two ranch hands heading into the barn. I let out a yawn and waved at them. I'd been out here for three and a half hours. I was cold, and my stomach let out a growl to remind me I still hadn't eaten.

Ella would have breakfast ready by now, I thought as I looked toward the house. I gave a couple of orders to the guys in the barn and then made my way up to the house. As I approached the back door, I heard the steady beeping of the fire alarm. I frowned, quickening my pace, and just before I climbed the steps to the door, I smelled burning bacon. I frowned. Ella was always attentive when she had food on the stove.

I pulled the back door open and entered the smoke-filled kitchen. Immediately, I grabbed a towel and moved the cast iron pan off the gas stove and into the sink. I shut the burner off and opened the window then took the towel and furiously waved it under the smoke alarm, trying to get the noise to stop. Finally, it let up. I went over to the sink and looked at the eight shrived pieces of burnt bacon in the pan. "What the hell," I muttered under my breath. The crispy sticks looked like they'd been in that pan for about an hour.

"Ella?" I yelled, listening as I waited for her to respond. "Ella?" I yelled again. When I heard nothing, I threw the towel on the counter and made my way into the living room, then into the bathroom. She wasn't there. I yelled from the bottom of the stairs, but again there was nothing.

I tried to think of anywhere else in the house she might be. As I made my way back into the kitchen, that was when I caught sight of her slippered feet lying on the floor of the pantry. Panic filled me as I pushed the door open to find my wife on the floor, a jar of jam broken beside her head. "Ella?" I muttered, rolling her over to find her eyes wide open, staring back at me.

I dropped to the floor, shaking her, but it did little good. She didn't respond. I stared into her eyes, an enormous mountain of dread filling me, and swallowed hard. Then, with shaking hands, I placed two fingers on the side of her neck, already knowing full well what I was going to find. The temperature of her skin told me all I needed to know, and I ripped my hand away from her, covering my mouth to stop my screaming.

One Month Later

I sat on the edge of our bed, looking down at the photo of us we had taken only a few months ago. It had taken me time to realize that my Ella was gone, and so was our unborn child. Autopsy reports had shown she'd had an aneurysm. I'd been filled with guilt that I hadn't been there, but the doctor told me there would have been nothing I could have done, even if I had been right there.

She ceased to exist in under a blink of an eye. Still, the guilt of not being there was eating me alive.

"Connor."

I looked up from the photo and saw my best friend, Gabe, standing in the doorway to what had been Ella's and my bedroom. I was thankful to have him. He'd stepped up and helped a lot over the past few weeks.

"I went over everything with my guys. Everyone knows their jobs for the next few weeks. You can take the time you need to heal, without worrying about this place."

I nodded. It had been hell the last few weeks. Gabe had been my rock, as he'd always been. He'd helped with the funeral arrangements and with the celebration of life. I'd never been so thankful to have him by my side. However, yesterday, he'd found out his grandmother passed away. He felt bad that he had to abandon me, and I felt bad that I couldn't return the favor and be stronger for him.

"Thanks. I appreciate it. When are you heading out?" I questioned, placing the photo I'd been looking at back down on the side table.

"Tomorrow."

I nodded. "What about your ranch? What about Cadence? She can't possibly look after it all while you are gone?"

Gabe looked at me and shook his head. "Connor, Cadence has been out with our grandparents for the past five years. Did you forget?" he asked, a frown lining his face.

I looked at my best friend. Perhaps I had forgotten that his sister had left. After all, the last month had been a blur. I'd seen people at the wake I hadn't seen in years, and now I couldn't figure out who hadn't been there. I was sure she'd been here. It wasn't just things like that I'd forgotten. I was forgetting little things, like putting gas in the tractor the other day before driving halfway across the cattle field only to have it stall out.

I frowned. "It's been a whirlwind this past month." I shrugged, not wanting to let on that I still wasn't coping very well. I wasn't sure why I felt the need to hide it. I was certain he already knew it, but I felt ashamed.

"I'm sure it has. No need to worry. I'll be back in a week. I have enough help at the house to make do, and you should be fine here now that I got three of my guys to help here."

"Thanks," I muttered, looking at my friend's saddened face. I felt helpless. Gabe had always done what he could to help me, and under different circumstances, I knew he knew he could count on me. "Have a safe trip."

"Thanks, man. Just get yourself some rest. I'll be back before you know it."

Connor

July 2023

I ran my dirt-covered hand through my messy hair. Sweat poured from my brow, and I wiped my forehead with the sleeve of my shirt. It was hot as hell out, and I couldn't wait to be done today. Without wasting any more time, I picked up the sledgehammer and began pounding another fence post into the ground. Fixing fences had been the chore for today. It was one field we hadn't used since the storm passed through shortly before Ella died. It was also the field closest to the house, and we'd need it for winter.

We needed it to be fixed and we also needed to repair the feed barn. I'd made do last winter, but this year, I feared the feed I'd begun storing would spoil if I didn't get a new roof on it. Which only fixed my mind on other issues, like where I'd get the money.

"Okay, guys, you can bring the wire up to here now," I called, moving to the next post.

Dropping the sledge on the ground in front of the next post, I made my way over to the back of my truck. Pulling my thermos from the back seat, I took a swig of the now warm water.

The days were already beginning to get shorter, and soon you'd be able to see a hint of colour in the leaves. Cold weather would be here before I knew it, as it always was. I looked off toward my driveway. A trail of dirt rose as a truck drove toward the house. It wasn't often we had visitors, especially now that Ella was gone. In fact, unless it was Gabe, visitors were non-existent.

"Looks like someone is coming to see you, Connor," Joey said as he fixed the wire on the post.

"Yeah, I guess." I shrugged, hammering the next post into the ground.

"We can finish up here. Go on."

"Are you sure you got this?" I asked, turning to Joey and the other two young guys I'd hired to work for me since I took the place over from my father. They'd been here when I'd purchased the cattle from Jenkins Ranch, right after Thomas's dad died. Shortly after, Ella and I married and got pregnant. Then we moved into the old farmhouse where we'd laid out our plans, and then 'life' stepped in and changed everything.

"Yep, you can inspect it tomorrow."

"No need. I'll come back out once I deal with whatever it is," I said, leaving the three of them to continue with the job at hand. Climbing into my truck, I took off toward the house.

As I pulled around beside the house, I noticed Gabe's truck sitting in the driveway, and then I saw him wave. He was sitting on the porch looking a little distraught, which caused me to wonder what was wrong. As I climbed out of the truck and made my way over to where he sat, I could see the tension in his face, in his body. Something was wrong, and it immediately set off alarms inside of me.

"What is it?" I asked, climbing the steps of my front porch and leaning up against the rail. I wasn't wasting time beating around the bush. I needed to know what was wrong.

"Jesus, Connor, look at yourself. Clean yourself up." Gabe chuckled, a smile coming to his face as he looked me over.

I looked down at my dirt-covered jeans and shook my head. "How do you think a rancher should look? Definitely not like you." Gabe's family had owned a multi-generational dairy farm, and he had enough hands to look after his entire place if needed. I didn't have the funds to even straighten up the place, never mind pay for any more help than what I already had. I could barely afford them. To be truthful, I was barely making ends meet. The bank had refused to lend me any more money until I paid what I was overdue on. I'd fallen behind on payments shortly after Ella had passed and hadn't been able to get caught up.

"Why, so I can look like you?" I chuckled, scratching my sweaty back against a beam that supported the covered porch.

Gabe laughed. "What's wrong with looking like me?"

"Nothing at all, pretty boy," I kidded. "What are you doing here?" I questioned, positive that it had to only be about nine in the morning. He should be on the farm, not out here at my place.

"Well, I came to talk to you. Mallory called. She wants me to come into the city for a few weeks. I told her I'd only come out to complete our separation, but apparently, she now wants to talk things over," Gabe said, using air quotes as he rolled his eyes.

"So, she changed her mind about the divorce?" I asked.

"I guess. I don't know for sure. She was vague on the phone, along with a lot of tears."

"I see. How long are you going to be gone for?"

"Well, I do not know how long this is going to take. Last she told me, she wanted a separation, so I gave it to her. Now, who the hell knows what she wants? Perhaps she has forgotten all the reasons she wanted one to begin with," Gabe said, letting out a sigh.

"I'd have told her you were busy. I mean, the woman knows you have a farm to run."

Gabe nodded. "Yeah, she does." He hung his head. "Which is part of the reason she left. She couldn't stand not being the centre of attention all the time."

I'd become cold since I lost Ella. Back when she was alive, there wasn't anything I wouldn't have dropped if she needed something. Now, the farm came first, that was it. There wasn't anything else, or anyone. Besides, watching Mallory walk out on Gabe shortly after his grandmother had passed a month ago had pissed me off. She knew he needed her.

"I need a favour, Connor."

"What's that?" I questioned, feeling my stomach growl. I hadn't had breakfast yet and was suddenly starving.

"I need you to take care of things at the farm while I'm gone. At least check on things, make sure the work is getting done."

I chuckled. "Look, I'm a rancher, yes, but I know absolutely nothing about dairy farms. The horses I can easily look after, but you're probably better to get your sister for this. Want something to eat?"

I opened the front door of the house and made my way into my kitchen, with Gabe trailing behind. I pulled the pack of fresh sausage out of the fridge along with eggs and pulled a clean pan out of the pile of dishes that sat in the one sink.

Gabe stepped into the kitchen and looked around. I knew he was judging me. He'd been doing it since Ella died. I wasn't the best at keeping the place clean, nor did I care. Most nights I was way too exhausted to eat, never mind clean up the place. I needed a place to put my head at night. That was it.

"No bacon?" Gabe questioned, sitting down.

That question six months ago would have stopped me in my tracks. Instead I just shook my head. "Nope, and we aren't getting on that topic again," I replied.

I still couldn't stand the smell of bacon cooking after stepping into the house the day I found Ella dead. In fact, my stomach turned the second I even caught a whiff.

"So, why can't Cadence look after things? She should be back home soon."

Gabe met my eyes. "Like all the women in my life, she's decided she isn't coming back from our grandparents'. I tried to get her to stay when she was here for Ella's funeral, but she refused. I tried again when I went out there a month later when Gramps died. I figured after Grams went, she'd be packing up, but now she claims she won't return. She says that the farm meant too much to Grandma and Gramps. She doesn't want to let it go."

I nodded, throwing the sausage in the hot pan. "At

least she has her shit figured out," I muttered, wiping my hands on my jeans. "You've got to give her that."

Gabe let out a laugh. "My sister does not have her shit figured out. That much I can tell you."

"Sure she does. She's going to make a go of it out on the dairy farm at your grandparents'. That's something."

"I know Cadence, and I know her well. She's hiding from something. Something here," Gabe replied. "I just can't figure out what it is."

"Probably from her brother's fucked-up ex-wife." I chuckled, not able to help myself.

Only Gabe didn't laugh. Instead, his face turned serious, which made me stop laughing. "Sorry, that wasn't called for."

"It's fine. I know Mallory isn't everyone's favourite person. I also know she pissed you off when she packed her shit and left."

That was putting it lightly. They'd met at school. I, for one, couldn't stand her, and I knew Cadence felt the same. She'd told me that many times. Mallory came from an affluent home on the outskirts of Willow Valley, and I'd told Gabe from the start that she'd never be happy with a farmer, but he insisted. Things went well for the first couple of years before Gabe took over his parents' farm here. Then the trouble started.

I quickly plated up the breakfast I'd cooked and

carried both plates to the table, setting one down in front of Gabe.

"I just need to know you can help me out for a bit. It won't take much of your time, I promise."

"No problem. We can go over a plan on Monday," I said, digging my fork into my food while Gabe did the same.

I lay on the couch Sunday night flipping through the channels, debating whether I should just go to bed. Morning came early, and not only did I have the cattle to tend to, but I also needed to visit Gabe. I flipped a few more channels, wiped my hand over my face, and switched the TV off. I was just about to climb the stairs up to the bedroom when I heard a knock on the front door.

I glanced at my watch and frowned. It was after nine. An odd time to have company, I thought, knowing few people from the town came out this way this late at night. Getting up, I walked over and opened the door to find Gabe standing there.

"What's up?" I questioned.

"Got a minute?" he asked, running his fingers through his already disheveled hair.

"Yep. Want a beer?" I asked, knowing from the look on his face that this was indeed a beer drinking situation.

"Please."

I grabbed two beers from the fridge and brought them out to the porch, where we sat down. "What's going on?"

He twisted the cap off the bottle and, in one quick minute, downed half the bottle. "I did something kind of stupid," he muttered.

"Okay." I took a long draw on the beer bottle, wondering what stupid thing Gabe could have done. I prayed Mallory hadn't come back to town, and that they hadn't fallen into bed together.

"Mallory called, told me she changed her mind again. Told me not to bother coming out."

I chuckled. "Un-fucking-believable," I muttered under my breath. "Let me guess, you confessed your love for her—yet again—and then begged her to take you back."

As much as I felt Gabe was like a brother to me, I absolutely hated seeing him so whipped by a girl that he'd literally beg for her to take him back. The bitch walked out on him when he needed her. That, in my book, would be where I drew the line. It irritated me when he told me he was going to talk to her. I'd told him time and time again just to draw the line, but he claimed it wasn't that easy. I begged to differ, but then I'd never get into a relationship with a girl like Mallory to start.

"No, I didn't beg her to take me back. It's worse than that. She went on and on the other day about how things would have been different had I stayed in the Army. I knew Ethan Alexander had invited his military buddies to do an enlistment call in Willow Valley a few weeks ago."

My eyes flew to my best friend. "Gabe, what the hell did you do?"

He was quiet for a few minutes, drinking his beer, then he looked over at me. "I was feeling pretty low after the call with Mallory. Call it my moment of weakness. I miss her, Connor. Anyway, I had to go into town, and well, I stopped at the hall and may have enlisted."

I glued my eyes on him, not believing what he'd said.

"I mean, it's not like I've never been in the military before." He shrugged. "I know what I'm in for."

"You did what?" I questioned, taking a large mouthful of beer myself. Gabe had joined the military when we'd been young guys, right after his mother had passed on. He'd been having a hard time coping. I could remember that Mallory was so proud that she was dating a military man. Anyway, he ended up leaving the Army because Cadence needed to go help her grandparents, and someone needed to help her father with the farm.

"It was stupid, I know, but at the time it felt right. Everything has gone for shit. I needed something familiar back in my life." He shrugged before taking another drink. "Plus, I figured, if it was needed, I could hit her back with the fact I'd gone back into military life. Sort of, I told you so."

I knew exactly how he was feeling. I knew how I felt after losing Ella; he didn't need to explain it. Hell, I'd grasped at everything for a while. "I get it. You feel lost. However, you have something familiar. What about the farm?" I asked, meeting my friend's eyes. "Besides, who the fuck cares what she thinks? She's a whiny, shallow bitch, man."

I never held back what I was feeling with Gabe. He didn't hold back either. It was part of why our friendship worked so well. If one of us didn't like something that was going on in our lives, the other said it. Nine times out of ten, the other agreed. We just needed the push to see what the other was seeing was right. It was how we each stayed in balance when things seemed off-kilter.

"I did and I still do. Anyway, I figured nothing would come of it, but last night, after I got off the phone with Mallory, I got a call. I'm being deployed on a peacekeeping mission after I finish re-training in a few weeks, and..."

"Here it comes," I mumbled, knowing exactly what was coming.

"This time, I really need you to look over the farm." Gabe looked at me, sadness lining his face. "I need this, Connor, you don't understand."

I leaned forward and rested my forearms on my knees and looked down at the boards on the porch. Gabe was wrong. I understood wholeheartedly. I just didn't know if I could do it. My hands were full here. There weren't many hours left in the day to do things.

"I know what you're thinking. You can't handle it all. I'm working on figuring that out. You are also right about Mallory. The minute I told her I was being deployed; her tune changed. She suddenly said she'd been wrong to tell me not to come, that she wanted to see me to work things out. That's why before I came over here, I dropped the signed papers from her lawyer in the mail."

I nodded.

"I'm glad you see it too, about Mallory." I nodded, taking another drink.

We both grew quiet as we looked out over the farmland. I'd help my friend, he knew it. I owed him after everything he'd done for me. There wasn't much more to say. Gabe knew I'd been struggling. That was why he'd been here daily since Ella had passed—to check on me. He may not know that I noticed, but I did. I couldn't get mad either. He was being a friend. The friend I needed.

"Are you going to be okay?" he questioned.

"What do you mean?"

"If I leave, are you going to be okay?"

I leaned back in my chair and nodded. "Do I have any other choice? She's been gone for over a year. It's time that I pick up the pieces and move on. I know you're worried. It's written all over your face, but I'll be fine."

"I know. I just feel like I'm abandoning you in your time of need. It's just..."

"It's just you have to do this for you. I get it, Gabe, I really do. Why do you think I do nothing but work? It's my way of coping. This is yours."

"I just wish your way of coping had changed."

"What is that supposed to mean?" I asked, emptying my beer.

"Oh, I don't know, perhaps you could cope by, getting involved with a woman. A relationship may do you good."

I looked off into the distance. "Nah, I don't think so," I muttered, getting up and returning with two more beers. The last thing I needed right now was to have a conversation about my personal life. Gabe should know better than to start on me about dating again.

"Sorry man, I just thought that it may help you cope with things."

I passed him another beer and sat back down. "Now I'll do what I can to help you out, but you say you are trying to figure something else out? Care to shed a little light on that subject?" I asked.

"I'm heading out to see Cadence, to see if I can convince her to return home. If she does, I know she'll need help. Our farm is twice the size of our grandparents'."

First, he started with my personal life and then he mentioned Cadence in the same sentence. He better not be thinking what I thought he was. I took another mouthful of beer and cleared my throat.

"You aren't suggesting that Cadence and I..."

Gabe shrugged and sort of smirked as he tipped the bottle back.

There had been a time that I'd had a crush on her, but she gave no hints. Then Gabe made it very clear to me and some other guys at school she was off-limits. In fact, I remembered him muttering something about the bro code after he gave another kid in town a black eye for hitting on his sister. After that, I knew better than to think about touching his sister, as did every guy in town. I enjoyed having my balls intact. Since I hadn't been willing to ruin our friendship, I pushed my feelings to the back of my mind and gotten involved with her friend Ella.

"Cadence, from what I remember, can look after herself," I muttered. "She's looked after your grandparents' farm just fine with no help from anyone. She doesn't need my help."

"Yeah, but it's different here. More moving parts, bigger operation, and I'd just feel better knowing that I can count on the only man I trust here to be there if she needs something," Gabe said, looking at me.

I chuckled.

"Please, Connor."

I hated seeing my friend beg, but at least he was begging me and not some woman who would only slap him across the face when he got close enough. I drank back the rest of my beer and nodded my head.

"Fine. Let me know once you figure it all out. I'll help her for a bit, but once Cadence is all settled in and things are going well, I'm done."

Cadence

Gabe stood on my front porch smiling back at me. "What are you doing here?" I asked as I looked at my brother.

"Can't I come out and visit my sis?"

I crossed my arms over my chest and looked at my brother, who now stood there with his arms open, waiting for a hug. When I didn't immediately step into his arms, he gave me a goofy smile instead. The one that told me he was here for different reasons other than just a friendly visit. "Can I at least come in out of the rain?"

I stepped to the side to let him in. It had been pouring hard most of the morning. So hard, in fact, that I cleaned up the kitchen and completed most of my housework before I even thought about going out to check on the cattle.

"I don't have a ton of time, Gabe. I have to get out and get started on all the daily chores that need to be done. So, are you going to tell me what exactly I did to earn a visit?" I asked, while grabbing the mop and dunking it into the pail of water that sat in the middle of the kitchen floor.

"I just thought it would be nice to come and visit. Can't a brother come and visit his sister?" Gabe asked as he leaned up against the counter. "Haven't seen you for a bit."

"Uh-huh. Although in the five years I've been here, you've never just come to visit me. Besides, since when has it mattered that you haven't seen me for a bit?" I wrang out the mop and began washing the kitchen floor.

He grew quiet, then met my eyes as I dropped the mop back into the pail. "Cadence, have you given any thought to returning to Willow Valley?"

I stopped dead. Was he kidding? He had to be kidding. Were we really back on this topic again? "I see you're not wasting time. At least you are getting right to the reason you are really here."

"Come on, Cadence," he said, leaning up against the counter.

"Gabe, I told you. My life is here now, not in Willow Valley. I've built it that way. I have friends here. I have a home here," I said, looking around the kitchen.

Gabe looked around the kitchen and crossed his arms. "Cadence, you can't be serious."

"Why not? This place is perfect for me. I'm happy here." The house was the same way it had been before Grandma passed. I hadn't done a thing to it, because in my mind it was perfect the way it was. Just not perfect for a woman who was only twenty-six.

"Cadence, this place needs updating. Besides, friends move. Are you still seeing that guy you were dating? Fuck, what was his name...?" Gabe questioned.

"Daniel?"

"That's it...yes. Are you still seeing him?"

"Not that it's any of your business, but no, I'm not. I haven't been for a while. Besides, what does he have to do with anything?"

Gabe shrugged. "Nothing. He has nothing to do with it. I was only thinking that it would be easier for you to move back home if you were indeed single."

"My home is here, Gabe. I told you once before and I'll tell you again. In fact, I'll tell you every time you bring it up, I'm not coming back to Willow Valley."

Gabe grew quiet while I once again rung out the mop and started washing the floor again. He cleared his throat, breaking the silence of the room.

"Cadence, I don't think you're understanding. I'm not asking."

I stopped and looked at my brother. Irritated beyond belief, I shoved the mop back into the bucket, this time spilling water out onto the floor. "Well it sure sounded like a question to me."

"It isn't a question. I need you to return home."

I stopped dipping the mop in and out of the water and turned away from my brother. Then my mind began spinning with horrible thoughts. Was he sick? Oh god, was he dying? Was it cancer? Not cancer. That's what took both dad and Gramps, and it was horrifying to watch. There was no way I could do it again. I couldn't watch that happen to him. He was so young, and he was the only family I had left. I looked over my shoulder at my brother, noticing a heavy look on his face. What on earth could cause that expression otherwise? Fear filled me as I silently prayed that he wasn't sick.

"Why?" I asked as I held my breath, afraid to move.

Gabe let out a breath, then ran his hand through his hair. "I've been called to go back to the Army. I'm heading on a peacekeeping mission in a few weeks. I need you, Cadence. The farm needs you."

"I thought you said you were done with the military." Relief flooded me as I leaned the mop against the counter and put my hands on my hips.

"I was."

"You were? Let me guess, it was, until the devil herself

dumped you?" I looked at my brother, who averted his eyes. "I'm right, aren't I. You're going back in because of her, because of Mallory."

"The reason doesn't matter. What matters is that you come back home and—"

I turned my back on my brother and walked across the small kitchen and looked out the back door window. I didn't want to go back. I'd fought so hard to leave that small town and the ghosts that I'd left there. My own ghosts and demons that every once in a while, appeared in my mind, haunting me. The most recent one from a year ago.

"Gabe, it's not that simple," I muttered. "This farm means a lot to me."

I could see Gabe nod out of the corner of my eye. He understood, or at least I hope he understood. "I get it, but the family farm...it's bigger. It produces a hell of a lot more than this. It can provide a much healthier income for you and—"

"This is all I need, Gabe. I don't need a large operation, just like I don't need a lot of things. I'm happy living this simple life. Besides, I promised them," I said, tears filling my eyes at the thought of selling this place to return to Willow Valley, to the place where I'd had my heart torn into pieces. The opportunity to leave there hadn't appeared until Grandma and Gramps needed help, and I'd been grateful for it. It came at a time that I couldn't stand looking at my face in the mirror. I also couldn't stand looking at my best friend or her boyfriend, a guy I'd had a crush on my entire teenage life. A guy who never even knew I existed.

Gabe turned around and made his way back to the front door. With his hand on the knob, he stopped. "Just tell me you'll think about it."

I said nothing. I just stood there. He didn't know what it was he was asking of me. It had been hard enough going back there to say good-bye to Ella, who had once been my best friend. A friendship that I allowed jealousy to overtake. He also didn't know it had taken me months to get myself back to a place of happiness after I'd returned from her funeral, especially after what had happened.

"Just tell me that. I'm going to go out to the barn and do some work. We can talk about it later."

He didn't wait; he opened the door and then closed it behind him, leaving me in the kitchen. I watched as he made his way out to the barn in the rain. There was something else in this ask. I just didn't know what it was, but I prayed it had nothing to do with Connor Darling.

I pulled Grandma's blue casserole dish from the oven and lifted the lid. The smell of delicious cheesy casserole filled the air. I'd taken the opportunity to make it, knowing that Gabe was here for dinner—at least for tonight. It wasn't very often I got to have Grandma's Cheesy Beefy Biscuit Casserole, and lately I'd been craving it. Plus, I'd needed something to occupy my mind, because once I'd started thinking of Connor, he'd invaded my thoughts the entire day.

"What on earth is that smell?" Gabe questioned, coming into the kitchen.

"Dinner," I said, pulling down two plates and placing them on the small table. "Grandma's Cheesy Beefy Biscuit Casserole."

Gabe walked over and lifted the lid, taking a smell. "I don't remember it smelling like that."

"That's because Grandma and I perfected it. Just wait till you taste it. It's better now."

Gabe grabbed two cans of soda from the fridge and brought them over to the table. I placed the dish on the table and shoved a large spoon into the mix, waiting while Gabe helped himself first, before taking some for me. I sat down and had just stuck my fork into the gooey mixture when Gabe looked over at me.

"Well, did you give what we talked about any thought?"

I let out a sigh. "Here we go... I figured I'd at least have the night to think it over, perhaps at least get through dinner. What's the rush?"

"Cadence, you act as if I don't have a timeline. I have to leave on their schedule, remember? I need you there when I leave. That means we need to act on getting this place up for sale. The cattle can come home with you."

"That goes without saying. Of course they'd be coming with me." I sat back and placed my fork down on my plate and scrunched my napkin in my hand. "Gabe...I just...there is something else, isn't there?" I said, looking at my brother. "I feel this is all too rushed. You want me there for another reason? It's not only because you are leaving?"

Our eyes locked as we sat in my small kitchen. He kept his eyes trained on me and then quickly averted them. He shook his head and stuck his fork into the meat and cheese, taking another mouthful before looking at me. "No," he said, his mouth still partially full.

I couldn't help but laugh. Did he really think I was this stupid? Gabe only ever spoke with his mouth full of food when he was lying. He'd done it since he was a kid. It used to piss off our father, and now it was pissing me off. "You better tell me or else..."

"Or else what?" he said, giving me a knowing look as he cracked open the can of soda in front of him and took a drink.

"Or else I won't go. You can't force me to sell something you don't own." I met my brother's eyes. I wasn't playing games anymore. He either needed to tell me everything or nothing was going to happen.

"Cadence."

I shook my head. "No, Gabe, I'm serious. You've hired enough people to manage everything on that farm, whether you are home or while you are gone. You already have help. It's not like it's just you. You don't really work; you oversee things now. So, there is no reason you can't put your top guy in place as a manager and have him check in with you. You don't need me there at all!" I stared into his eyes. "Why is it so important that I come back to Willow Valley?"

Gabe leaned back against his chair, ran his hand over his face, and then let out the breath he was holding. "Don't kill me."

I frowned. "What?"

"You're right. It's not just about helping me with the farm while I'm away."

"I knew it," I said, slamming my small fist down on the table. "So you've lied to me?" I questioned, feeling irritated. Gabe could barely look me in the eye now. I'd known there was something else.

Gabe shook his head. "I wouldn't say lied, just maybe didn't give you the entire picture." He gave me a crooked smile.

I focused on my plate, on the food that once had

looked so good. If I looked at my brother, I feared I may punch him. I knew there was something more. Something else he wasn't telling me. I swore if he uttered the words 'Connor Darling,' I'd scream.

"It's Connor," he said, as if on cue.

I gripped my fork so tightly in my hand, I was sure that my knuckles were white.

"So, no, it's not just about helping me. I've asked him to look over the farm, but I'm worried about him. Ever since Ella died, he's not the same."

"Why would you expect he'd be the same? It was tragic. It was horrible. Losing both your wife and your soon-to-be child at the same time. I can't even imagine the pain he must have felt."

"I know. However, the only time I see even a glimmer of the man he once was, was when he is around me. The only other time was when you were back at the house for the funeral. I just fear that if I leave, he will really retreat into himself. He isn't getting better. He needs to be surrounded by those that love him."

"There was no glimmer of the man he once was when I was at that funeral, Gabe. He was a disaster. So, tell me, exactly how do I fit into this, because I'm failing to see how me being there will help him?"

I waited for Gabe's response. When he said nothing, I got up from the table and dumped my plate into the sink.

Was he suggesting that perhaps I go back and that Connor and I...?

I cleared my throat and turned back to face my brother. "You aren't suggesting what I think you are?" I questioned.

He smirked. I let out a huff and wiped my hands on the towel that sat on the counter and, without looking at my brother, I left the room. He wouldn't dare suggest what I was thinking. At least he'd better not be.

"Aren't you going to eat?" he called from the kitchen as I stood at the bottom of the stairs.

"Lost my appetite, thanks. Enjoy your dinner!" I yelled back and climbed the stairs.

It was well past my bedtime, yet I couldn't sleep.

Once I'd left the kitchen, I'd gone out to the barn and sat with the cows. I'd finally come in and watched some TV alone, then I'd gone up to my room, only to come back down once I knew Gabe was in bed. Now, I sat in the living room, in the dark, holding a cup of hot tea while my brother slept soundly in our grandparents' bedroom.

I stood up and grabbed the blanket off the end of the

couch and wrapped it around me then sat back down. I took a mouthful of warm liquid and closed my eyes. It had been a year since I'd been in Willow Valley, and yet I hadn't been able to get what had happened out of my mind. The memory was as clear as day in my mind, and if I thought hard enough, I could still feel the feelings I'd had.

I stood in the kitchen washing dishes. I was sure Ella's parents had used every serving dish and platter Connor and Ella owned. It had been a nice celebration of life, I thought as I placed more dishes into the sink to soak, while scrapping little remnants of food off others. Once finished, I wiped down the counter I'd finally cleared and went back to the sink, carefully washing each dish.

Ella's parents were thankful I'd come. After all, they'd been like parents to me growing up. Ella was like the sister I hadn't had.

"Cadence, love. Thank you for coming. Ella talked about you all the time. She would be happy to know you were here," Mrs. Connor said to me as she carried another load of dishes into the kitchen.

"Of course. I had to be here," I said. I blinked away the tears that blinded my eyes and quickly wiped them away. I hadn't spoken to Ella since they'd gotten married, and now I regretted my decision to allow my feelings to tear apart my friendship.

"It was good to see you. Mr. Connor and I are going to

head out soon. It's been a long day and there are only a few guests left. We are both—"

"No need to say anything," I said, cutting her off before she could say any more. "It's been hard on everyone," I muttered, walking over and throwing my arms around her neck.

"You will keep in touch, won't you? I mean, just because Ella is..." She hugged me tighter as she broke down into tears once again.

I fought back my own tears and pressed my lips to her cheek. "Don't you worry, I'll always be here. We can even set up a call every week if you like. We can even do it through Zoom. That way, we can be face-to-face."

She ran her hands over the back of my head, smoothing my long hair, just like she'd done when I was a kid. "I'd love that, Cadence."

"Paula, we should get going," Mr. Connor said, stepping into the kitchen, giving me a sad smile.

I gave her one last hug and watched as Mr. Connor wrapped his arm around her, guiding her out of the kitchen. I turned and walked back over to the sink and was about to put my hands into the hot water when tears fell from my eyes. I'd held it together the entire day, until now. Guilt now consumed me. I hadn't spoken to Ella in four years, aside from the occasional email. I'd been so devastated when Connor and she had announced their engagement, I'd had no choice but to cut ties. I'd even refused to be her maid of honour, using my grandparents as an excuse. I never came to her baby shower either. Now, I'd never speak to her again.

I heard the door swing open. "Cadence, how's it going in here?" my brother asked, dropping a garbage bag just outside the back door.

"Fine. Just about finished. You?"

"Okay. I've got to run a couple of people back to the inn for Connor. You be okay here while I do that?"

Did I have a choice? I'd told him I'd help with the cleanup. I didn't back down on my word. "I'll be fine. How long will you be gone?"

Ignoring my question, he came up and put his arm around me. "Oh, and when you're finished, Connor is out on the front porch. Go talk with him. He told me he wanted to see you. Probably wants to thank you for all you've done today."

I gripped the cloth in my hand and nodded. "Fine. You be back soon?" I asked again.

"No longer than an hour. See you then."

I finished up the last bit of the dishes, washed down the counters, and made my way into the living room. Everything was back to normal. The house was quiet once again and almost everything was back in its place. I walked over to the wall where they kept all their framed photos and looked at my best friend's wedding picture. They both looked so happy, and suddenly I was sad I missed seeing the day they got married.

I looked around the room, spotting many pictures of them on the mantel above the fireplace. I walked over and looked at each one of them, and then I spotted one of Ella and me. I smiled. It was from the fall fair the year before they'd started dating. I had the same one, only I'd shoved it away, sure that Ella would have done the same. Six months later, she'd started dating Connor, and we'd had our big fight. The one that started the decline in our friendship.

I heard something and turned to see Connor standing out on the porch. His hands rested on the wooden railing as he looked out over the cattle fields. I sucked in a breath. I'd not said a word to him all day because it was easier for me to avoid him. The house had been full of people vying for his attention, anyway. With everyone here, I'd been able to duck in and out of the room without being seen, but now I had no choice.

I sucked in a breath and made my way to the door. Pushing it open, I stepped outside, the cool night air hitting my warm skin. Connor didn't move. Instead, he stood there, his large muscular hands gripping that wooden railing, every muscle in his body tense.

"Connor?" I said, my voice low. "Gabe said you wanted to talk to me once I finished cleaning up everything?"

He said nothing, but he turned to reveal his gorgeous blue eyes, red and full of tears. I didn't move. I could barely breathe, and it felt like I was glued to the spot in which I was standing. He stared at me for a moment, then made his way over to me. Without warning, he wrapped his arms around me and pulled me into him. Ever so slowly, I allowed my arms to wrap around him, my hands to land on his strong back. It was then I felt his body shake. I wrapped my arms around him and held him tight. He'd not broken down once during the day, so it did not surprise me he had now.

We stood there for a long time, holding one another. It was when he backed away from me and we made eye contact that something changed. It was the most intense look I'd ever seen; so intense I could feel it. Instead of pulling away from me like he should have, his lips crashed into mine.

I wiped the tears from my eyes as I sat in the dark. As all the times before when I thought about that moment, I could still feel his body against mine, and I could remember feeling angry and jealous. She'd gotten to experience what it had been like with him. In all ways. The fun ways, the tender ways, the intimate ways, while all I got was to comfort him after she was gone. The entire time I hugged him that evening, along with that one kiss that ended faster than it had started, all I could think about was how much I hated her.

There were so many reasons I didn't want to return to Willow Valley. He was only part of it. I was the other part. I'd never let go of that hate toward her. I also had to contend with the anger toward my brother. He never would have allowed me to date any of his friends, especially Connor, and now, it seemed, he was encouraging it. Throwing us together in some terrible experiment. I ran my hand through my hair and looked at the clock. It was almost three; I had to be up in an hour.

I placed my mug down on the table and leaned back against the couch. I hoped I could look at things a little differently in the morning, and I'd try.

I'd just thrown the blanket down on the back of the couch when I heard the bedroom door open and looked to see Gabe step out, his hair a mess. "What are you doing up?" he questioned, his voice thick with sleep.

"Thinking," I muttered. It wasn't odd that my brother was up. He was always early to rise.

"I see." He came over and sat down, running his hands through his messy hair. "What about?" He yawned.

"What you asked me."

"Ah, I see. And..."

I closed my eyes and leaned back against the couch. Gabe never knew about my crush on Connor, and now didn't seem to be the time to tell him. He also didn't know about that kiss that night. He also didn't know that as his truck was roaring up the driveway, Connor followed me into the house, apologizing profusely, begging me not to tell Gabe. Yet he needed to know what I thought he was trying to do.

"Gabe, I'd come home for you anytime. This Connor

stuff, well, to be honest, I don't want to be Connor's second choice," I blurted out, not really caring what the hell my brother thought.

Gabe looked at me, rubbed his eyes, then leaned back against the couch. "Cadence, you aren't his second choice, but I believe you just might just be his second chance, because right now, the man is completely dead inside."

Cadence

August

It had taken me a couple of weeks to pack up and to get in touch with an agent willing to put up Gram and Gramps' place on the market. The house needed work, and Gabe said he'd pay for all the renovations and updates if I was moving back. He'd even hired the crew to take care of everything. All I had to do was manage it. Once the renovations were finished, the agent I'd hired would list the property, and the plan was to have it sold by Christmas.

I'd left the hotel I'd spent the night at and had just filled the tank with gas. When Gabe left two weeks ago he'd taken the cattle and my cattle trailer. He said it would be easier for him as he'd drive straight through. He also told me it would give me the opportunity to take my time and not stress about making the drive, if I'd decided to come back home. He wanted to make it as stress free and as easy as possible for me.

I climbed into my truck, placing the cold pop I'd just bought in the holder. I reached into the bag and pulled out the bag of chips and ripped it open. It wasn't the best lunch I could have bought, I thought to myself as I popped two chips into my mouth and started the engine.

I pulled away from the pump and back out onto the street, noting the sign for Willow Valley only a few more hundred miles. I turned on the radio and searched until I found some music I liked and settled in for the rest of the drive.

Almost three hours later, I pulled onto the road that led into Willow Valley. I blew out a breath as my stomach hitched. I'd given it thought on my drive out. The Willow Valley Bed and Breakfast would be fine to stay at while Gabe was gone, I thought to myself. It was easier than moving back into our parents' house.

"And more expensive, too." Gabe's words ran through my mind as I drove through Willow Valley.

I finally pulled into the driveway of the bed and breakfast, surprised to see that the place looked closed. I frowned. I could see a note on the door, so I climbed out of the truck and made my way to it, where my stomach sank.

Because of personal family issues, the Willow Valley Inn will remain closed until further notice. Sorry for the inconvenience. Sincerely, Bessy Tulip.

I climbed back down the stairs and looked around at the small town. This wasn't how this was supposed to go. I was supposed to get a room far enough away, but close enough that I could run and check on things.

I climbed back into my truck and drove down to The Crispy Biscuit. I wasn't sure if getting food would be a wise idea because, suddenly, I felt very sick to my stomach. The matter only intensified when I stepped foot into the small diner.

The owner, Brooke, stood behind the counter, a large smile on her face as her eyes landed on me.

"Cadence! It's so nice to see you."

I smiled. I wasn't used to this small-town life anymore. Everyone knew everything about each other. There were barely any secrets, and when one person found something out, it spread like wildfire.

"You too."

"What can I get for you? Did you want to have a seat?" she questioned, grabbing a menu.

I nodded. I wanted to take as much time as possible before getting to my brother's place. She led me over to a booth against the wall and left me with the menu, finally returning with a hot cup of coffee.

"So, Gabe told me you were moving back here. It's nice to have another familiar face back in town," she said, taking a seat across from me.

"Thanks. Yeah, it will be a change."

"I was sorry to hear about your grandparents."

I smiled. "Thank you. Yes, it was hard, but they are both in a better place now," I said, looking down at the menu.

"And about Ella. I know you two were so close. I still remember you both coming in after school when you were younger."

I smiled, not wanting to be rude. "Yes, we were close."

"Gosh, and Connor, poor man. He hasn't been the same since. Not that I'd expect him to be. The entire town mourned for him. I can still see his face when he came in the morning they'd found out about the baby. He was so excited. He bought coffee for the entire diner, along with sweets." She softly smiled.

I nodded. If she didn't stop, I knew I would either cry or get angry. I cleared my throat and picked up the mug, taking a sip of hot coffee.

"Then when we heard the news that she hadn't been well, we all did what we could to help. Unfortunately, it wasn't enough. I still remember seeing him for the first time after it had happened. It was like someone had sucked the life from him."

I couldn't hear any more. I remembered seeing the sadness on his face. It had almost killed me. I just couldn't. I placed the menu down on the table and met Brooke's eyes. "You know, I think I'll have the eggs, home fries, and toast with sausage."

I wanted her to stop talking; I didn't want to hear any of this. I certainly didn't want her to ask me questions regarding Ella.

"Okay, great. Well, it's nice to see you back in town," she said, standing up and making her way over to the counter where she placed my order and then started serving some walk-in customers.

I took my time eating, and once I'd finished, I quickly paid the bill and left. I was sure that by the time I drove out to Gabe's, the entire town would know I was back. I would need to get used to that again. As I hopped into my truck, I could tell it was already starting. Trinity was standing outside of The Crispy Biscuit with another lady talking to Brooke, the three of them looking in my direction. I blew out a breath, started my truck, and pulled away from the curb.

It was Monday. I'd gotten up early, as always, and had done half a day's work out on my ranch before sunrise. Then I'd gone inside, showered, eaten, and then made my way over to Gabe's. I'd been helping him steadily every day since he returned from seeing Cadence. We hadn't talked about the outcome of his visit, or if she was going to return. I'd just known he didn't seem to be overly happy when he returned, so I'd assumed that she'd told him no. Shortly after he'd gotten back, the military had extended his departure date, which had given me more time to learn more things from him. I'd been grateful for that. I hated being unsure of the things that needed to be done.

Music blaring on the radio, I drove down the long driveway toward his house. I was about to park my truck in my usual spot right behind him but couldn't. An unfamiliar truck sat parked there instead. Had he found someone to manage the farm? God, I hoped so. Every night since I'd started helping him, I'd gone home exhausted.

My body ached as I climbed out of my truck. I was hoping for less pressure, and perhaps I was going to get the good news today. As usual, I walked up the steps to the front door, knocked, and walked inside.

"Gabe? You ready to get to work?" I yelled.

"Come in and grab a coffee!" he shouted from somewhere in the house. "Be down in a minute."

I didn't have time for a coffee. I wanted to get to work, but I stepped inside anyway. I was about to make my way into the kitchen when I heard the clinking of utensils. It hadn't sounded like he was in the kitchen. Perhaps he was finishing up some sort of lunch meeting with his new manager, I thought to myself—not that he or I held many of those. I stepped through the door to the kitchen, expecting to find Gabe. Instead, my eyes landed on curvy hips in a pair of jeans.

I allowed myself to look. Something I rarely had done since Ella had died. To follow the curves of those hips, down to the floor, then back up. Then the woman turned to the side. It was just enough that when she reached forward, I caught a peek at the curve of her large breast in her shirt. Had Gabe been holding out on me? Did he have a friend with benefits he hadn't told me about? That would be enough to piss Mallory off, I thought to myself. I was about to clear my throat and introduce myself to this incredibly sexy woman when she spun around. Immediately, I raised my hand, waiting for her to shake it, only to encounter a pair of green eyes I'd know anywhere.

My hand slowly dropped to my side as she looked at me. "Cadence?" I questioned; my voice low.

When I'd last asked, Gabe still hadn't alluded to whether she'd return. For that, I'd been grateful. I didn't know how the hell I'd work side by side with her day after day, anyway. Not because we didn't get along, because we did, but because of the secret I'd held from him since I was in my teens.

It was only because of Gabe I'd ever started dating Ella to begin with. It had really been Cadence I was interested in. Instead, I sucked it up, went on a few dates with Ella. After a bit of a rocky patch, and realizing I'd needed to let go of the dream I had of having Cadence as mine, we ended up falling in love and, well, here we are.

I'd never told another soul about this, but I'd crushed on Cadence badly. I'd wanted her then, and now there really wasn't anything that was stopping me. The last time I'd seen her had been at Ella's funeral. I barely remembered that day. It had been a fog, and I'd barely noticed half the people there. The only one I remembered being there had been Cadence. Her soft smile, the way she spoke to everyone, the way she'd looked at me. Then Gabe left us alone. We'd shared a kiss—a kiss that shouldn't have happened, but it had. I'd been feeling so dead inside that, just for a minute, I wanted to feel something again—anything. Even though it was completely inappropriate, I'd done nothing but think about it for months. When I heard Gabe's truck roaring up the driveway, I'd pulled away and apologized profusely. She, of course, nodded, said it was okay, and then ran off into the house. An hour later, she was gone, and that was the last time I'd seen her.

Just like that night, she didn't respond. Instead she walked across the kitchen, opened a cupboard, and pulled a mug out, placing it down in front of the coffeemaker.

"Would you like a coffee?" she questioned, turning again and meeting my eyes. "Gabe just had to run upstairs to get changed. A little barn mishap."

"Sure." I removed my hat and held it in my hands, pulled out a chair, and sat down before making eye contact with her again. "Is that your truck in the driveway?"

She glanced at me over her shoulder and nodded, giving me a small smile. "It is. It's good to see you, Connor."

I couldn't smile, and I couldn't tear my eyes off her. The room was full of tension, and I could barely breathe. "How about we skip the coffee, Cadence, and go straight for a whiskey? What do you say?" I grumbled, thinking back to that night and that kiss. I wondered how many times she'd thought about it over the last year. I wondered how many times she'd regretted it. Part of me did, but I felt a larger part of me did not. I also knew that the worst part about it was the fact I said nothing to her. Sure, I'd apologized, but I hadn't been able to explain myself.

Cadence tore her eyes from mine and pushed herself off the counter. "On second thought, I think I'll just go on out and check on the cattle. Maybe the horses too," she whispered, hanging her head as she pushed the back door open.

I pinched my brow. Ever since Gabe had mentioned Cadence to me, I'd thought about her. About what it might be like to have her back here. I'd even hoped that perhaps having her back here maybe in some ways would waken me from the nightmare I'd been living since Ella died. Give me the chance to feel alive again. It had worked once before. I just wanted the chance to feel anything again. It was as if I were on autopilot, and everything I did was because it needed to be done.

I got up from where I sat and wandered over to the back door. I watched as she made her way to where Gabe kept her horse. She then went over and grabbed a few apples off the one tree in the back, carrying them over to her horse. Climbing up on the lower rung of the fence, she held out the apple. The horse made its way over to her, taking the apple from her, and she rested her head on his.

I heard footsteps behind me and turned just in time to see Gabe step into the kitchen. "Cadence, did you get Connor a coffee?" he asked, looking around. "Where the hell is she?" he questioned, annoyance in his voice. "Ask her to do one thing and she bails."

"It would have been nice to have a warning," I gritted, taking one last look at her before turning to Gabe.

"Warning for what?"

"Last you said, she wasn't coming back," I said, running my hands through my almost dry hair.

Gabe chuckled. "Yeah, I know. However, I brought the cattle back here with me. She didn't want me to and said she would probably come back and get them. However, she showed up late last night, with all her shit inside." Gabe shrugged. "No warning."

"Wonderful," I muttered, more to myself than to him.

"Is there something wrong with her being back here?" Gabe asked, shifting his stance and crossing his arms over his chest.

"No," I abruptly answered. "Just..."

The room grew quiet as we stood there facing one another. I knew he was waiting for me to finish what I was going to say. Instead, he gave me a smirk and cleared his throat.

"I'm glad she came to her senses. I needed her here. It took a lot of convincing. You don't even know. Hell, she spent five years caring for our ailing grandparents. She was alone there and still is. What if I go on this mission and I don't come back? Last she needs to find out is that I got killed and that she'd need to come back home under those circumstances."

"True, but why not tell her that?" I said, sitting down with a mug of coffee. "Why not just be open and honest with her, instead of building up some false idea in her mind?"

"I can't tell her that. She'll flip out. I told her there wasn't any danger in me going. I'd rather her back here, with people she knows and can trust, than in the Midwest, alone, if she gets the call. Plus, if anything happens, I want to know she's taken care of, that the farm is self-supporting. My grandparents' place, while self-supporting, didn't make enough to keep her comfortable. I've been sending her money for almost a year to help pay for things."

I crossed my arms over my chest and looked at my best friend. "What the hell do you want from me, then? I mean, clearly she can look after this place on her own. Hell, she's been dealing with your grandparents' place all alone."

Gabe shook his head. While he knew damn well that Cadence was completely independent and could look after anything that came her way, there was still something he needed to say. I could see it in his eyes.

"Gabe, just spill it. I don't have the time for these games."

"Connor, I need you to promise that you'll look after her. That you'll help her around here. That if something should happen to me..."

"Nothing is going to happen to you, so cut the crap," I said, sitting back down at the table. I could feel his eyes on me, staring into me as he waited for me to say something else. Exactly what did he mean by looking after her? I cleared my throat and met his eyes. "The farm I can manage, but what exactly do you mean by look after her?"

Gabe said nothing. Instead, he made his way to the back door and looked outside. Then he cleared his throat. "Connor, it's been over a year."

I frowned. Was he seriously going to talk to me about a relationship with his sister? Did he know about the kiss we'd shared? Had she told him? Had I ever let it slip to him how much I'd liked her while growing up? I searched my mind, praying I hadn't mentioned it to him one night while we'd been drinking.

"What is that supposed to mean exactly? It wouldn't matter if it had been ten years, Gabe. What are you getting at?"

Still searching my mind for any memory of telling him, my mind instantly went back to that kiss. It never should have happened. I knew that. It was my wife's celebration of life! What had I been thinking? What sort of man was I? If anything I had ever done deserved a punch, it was that, and I knew Gabe would be the one to straighten me out if he ever found out.

"We'll talk about it later," Gabe said. "We've got to get to work."

"Not so fast. Sit down."

Gabe looked at me, afraid to move. He sat down across from me and looked me in the eye. "What?"

"Don't what me, Gabe. Tell me exactly what you meant by take care of her."

Gabe looked around the kitchen. He was on edge. I could see it. He shifted from one side to the other, then looked at me, nothing but concern in his eyes.

"I wasn't trying to be an ass when I said it's been a year. I've just given it a lot of thought, and before I go, I want to know if my sister is in good hands. If you catch my drift. She's never really had a good guy in her life, and I know you could be that for her."

What the fuck? Was he serious? Was he really sitting here telling me to get involved with her, when all those years ago, it was her I'd wanted, and he was the only reason I'd never had her?

I met his eyes, trying to figure out if he was serious. When his look didn't falter, I knew he was telling me the truth. He was giving me permission to date her. I allowed the idea to run through my mind. There was no way I could do it. No way I could betray Ella that way. I wasn't ready for anything, and everyone would agree. I got up from where I was sitting, tucked the chair back in under the table, and placed my mug in the sink.

"We should get started. I really need to get out there, get this work done. I have to be back home by three for a delivery," I mumbled as I walked out the door, leaving Gabe alone at the table.

Cadence

I stood on the cross member of the fence, watching my horse as she took another apple from my hand. I couldn't believe I was back in Willow Valley. Yet here I was. I heard the back door slam and watched as Gabe and Connor made their way out toward the cattle barn, neither of them looking in my direction. Connor looked irritated as Gabe tried to catch up to him.

I felt like I was sixteen again, watching them follow my father toward the barn. The only similarity between then and now was the fact that I still couldn't take my eyes off Connor Darling. He was different now. Bigger, broader shouldered, stronger, older. He'd gone from a boy to a man. As my eyes lingered, it was then he glanced in my direction. I averted my eyes quickly and spoke to my horse.

"It's been a long time, Ember," I said. "You're looking good. Soon I'll get you saddled up and we will take a ride out into the fields like we used to." I patted her head. "Would you like that?"

I'd missed riding my horse. I'd left her here when I went out to my grandparents'. They hadn't had the room to care for a horse, and I knew I'd be too busy to get her the exercise she needed anyway. I had thought this would be the best place for her to stay. I'd been right.

She let out a snort and shook her head. I reached for the last apple I'd picked and held it out for her to take.

I looked off toward the cattle barn in time to see Connor and Gabe step out of the door. It had crushed me to know that Connor wasn't happy to see me. I didn't know if I should be mad at Gabe for not telling him I'd returned or grateful so that I could see his actual reaction. I didn't know why I was so upset. I really didn't know how to expect the reunion to go, but in my mind, this hadn't been it.

Somewhere in my head, I'd worked it out that he would've opened his arms and wrapped them around me, pulling me into him. That I'd get to feel his hard body against mine and smell his cologne again. Then we'd both hug, smile, and laugh at some silly memory we'd once shared. Maybe if I'd been lucky, he'd have lowered his lips to mine and gently kissed me, nibbling or sucking a little on my bottom lip. Instead, he'd looked almost sick, gutted at the fact I was back.

Connor had changed. He looked older than his twenty-seven years. His eyes still held onto such sadness that it broke my heart. He'd once been so playful, so full of life, and now, it seemed, he'd aged years in a short time. I guess tragedy had a way of doing that to people. I'd seen it with Grams after Gramps left us. It really shouldn't have surprised me.

I went back up to the house and made my way up to my room. I watched from the upstairs window as Connor and Gabe worked out in the fields beyond the barn, each of them laughing at something the other had said. I sighed and turned to look at the things I'd left in my old room.

My small desk was still against the wall in my bedroom. A picture of Ella and me sat in the corner. I flipped the frame down, not wanting to feel her judging eyes on me. I didn't know how I was supposed to feel. Part of me still hated her. She'd gotten what I'd wanted. It was the same way I'd felt the night of her celebration of life. It was the way I'd felt right after they'd started dating and why I'd been in such a rush to leave Willow Valley. The feelings only grew more with each reminder I'd been given. Her wedding, the baby shower, her death, and then yesterday at The Crispy Biscuit. Perhaps it wasn't anger, perhaps it was regret at throwing away our friendship over something that seemed so silly. All I knew was that I was holding onto some toxic feelings that needed to be released.

I flopped down on my bed. I closed my eyes and thought back to the summer before college. Gabe, Connor, Ella, and I had driven out to Willow Valley Lake after we'd gone for ice cream. Connor parked his dad's truck, and the four of us climbed out. He'd grabbed two blankets from the back of the truck, along with towels, and the four of us took off toward the lake for an evening swim.

Ella and I set up the blankets and snuck behind the bushes to change into our swimsuits, while Gabe and Connor waited for us at the water's edge.

"You're sure you want to do this?" Ella asked, slipping on her bathing suit bottoms under her skirt.

"Yeah, I just know Gabe's thoughts on dating his friends." I giggled. "That's why I need you to distract him for me."

"Cadence, your brother isn't very easy to distract," Ella answered, while I slipped on my bathing suit bottoms.

"He likes you, Ella, I know he does. I've seen the way he looks at you," I said, hoping and praying that my plan worked.

"I'll do my best, but remember, if you get my signal, we'll have to move to Plan B."

"What's Plan B?"

Ella shrugged. "I don't know. I'm not sure I even know what Plan A is. But we can figure it out for next time."

We both laughed. I was so nervous, I couldn't stop shaking.

By the time we'd changed and made our way over to the blankets with our clothes, the guys were already in the water. "Come on, you two. Get in here!" Gabe yelled.

Together, we made our way over to the water's edge and got in. We swam around, took turns using the tree swing, and once it got dark, we all climbed out of the water. Once we'd all changed, I'd made my way over to the truck with our wet gear to grab the cooler from the back. I'd told Ella that after we got changed, I'd call Connor for help to get the cooler from the back. That was when Ella would distract Gabe and, fingers crossed, Connor would accept my advances.

Everything had gone as planned. I took the bags of wet suits over to the truck and pretended to try and get the cooler down. Then, after a few minutes, I called for Connor's help. Only instead of Connor, Gabe showed up.

"Hey, sis, let me get that for you," he said.

I frowned. Why hadn't Connor come? "Okay," I muttered, forcing a smile onto my face. What else was I supposed to do? He went right to work unhooking the cooler and sliding it out of the back of the truck with ease, while I stood there, frowning.

He carried the cooler, while I trailed behind him. Inter-

nally, I pouted that somehow something had gone wrong, and Ella wasn't able to get my attention since I'd left with the suits. Gabe was talking away when we'd come around the front of the truck, and that was when I saw Connor place his large hand on Ella's cheek.

My heart sank as I watched her kiss him back and then pull away, her eyes still closed. She smiled as she looked up at him and nodded her head. That was when she slipped her hand in his.

"What the hell is she doing?" I muttered under my breath.

My brother turned around and looked at me. "What did you say?" he questioned, looking back over at Connor and Ella before turning back to me.

"Is something wrong?" I could feel his eyes on me, and when I said nothing, he chuckled. "I know. An unlikely match, right. Connor is the only one of all my friends who is single. He said he was tired of being the third wheel, so...I suggested Ella. It's great, isn't it!"

Great! How on earth could it be great? It was horrific. My best friend had just kissed the guy I'd been crushing on for years, and it was all thanks to my brother.

"I'll be right bac., I...I forgot something," I mumbled, ripping my eyes from what I'd just seen, turning back toward the truck. If I didn't, I'd break down on the spot.

"All right, you know where to find us," Gabe said, as if nothing had happened. I'd taken a couple of steps away

from where they all stood, and that was when I heard Connor yell out, "She said yes, man!"

In the distance, I heard Gabe and Connor exchange a high five, while Gabe congratulated them. This had been their plan all along. This entire night was for Connor and Ella to get together.

I took off toward Connor's truck, and once I got there, I stood outside the passenger-side door, fighting back tears. All I wanted to do was go home. I swallowed hard to chase away the tightness in my throat as my eyes watered. When I heard footsteps on the gravel, I pulled the door open and reached into the back seat, pretending to be getting something.

"Cady...I..." Ella whispered as she placed her hand on my shoulder.

I couldn't turn around. I couldn't face the person who I'd thought was my friend. I'd felt so betrayed. She knew how much I liked him, yet she just stood there and accepted the kiss like it had come from some stranger.

"There it is," I said, my throat tight, pulling out my brother's hooded sweatshirt. "I was cold, and I forgot to grab it." My voice was thick, and I quickly wiped my eyes to make sure that tears hadn't fallen.

"It's not what you think, Cady. Please let me explain," she said, grabbing my arm.

I thought for a moment. There was no way I could cause a scene here. I needed to pretend to be happy for my best friend. So, I turned and looked my best friend in the eyes, a smile on my face.

"I'm thrilled for you," I lied.

"Cady..."

I held up my hand and began making my way back toward where the guys had built a small fire. "Really, Ella, I'm happy for you both," I said once again, over my shoulder, as we made our way over to the guys.

We sat there that night, around the fire, with me beside my brother while my best friend sat in the arms of the guy I'd had a crush on for years. It was a shitty thing to do on her part and something I doubted I'd ever be able to forgive. I also knew that just from watching them together, that perhaps I'd missed that she, too, felt the same way I did about him. That was the night our friendship changed forever.

I heard the door slam downstairs, pulling me from my memory. I hadn't thought about that night for years, and really there was no point in thinking of it now. Ella was gone. I sat up, taking a minute before I got up.

"Cadence, can you come down here?"

I frowned. That was Connor's voice. I got up from the bed and made my way down into the kitchen to see him standing against the counter.

"What's up?" I asked, acting as if I hadn't just been thinking of the night Ella betrayed me. I walked over to the sink and looked out the window to see my brother closing the barn door.

"Listen, I think maybe the two of us should send Gabe off with a good-bye dinner. Do you think you can throw something together for tomorrow night?" he asked.

I looked at Connor and then out the window at Gabe. He was still struggling with the latch on the door. "Yeah, I'll figure something out," I muttered, turning the water on to wash my hands.

That was when Connor stepped up beside me and slid his large, dirty hands under the running water. He looked me directly in the eyes as he rubbed his hands together. "Look, Cadence, I want to apologize."

"What for?" I questioned.

"For earlier. For what I said, how I acted." He cleared his throat.

Was he apologizing because my brother had told him to? Had they had it out while they were working outside, after I was out of earshot? I frowned. I'd need to drop this tough exterior shell I'd allowed to build around me as protection, if this working arrangement was going to have any chance of working.

I bumped his shoulder with mine and smiled. "No worries, big guy," I said, almost not believing my voice. It had a flirty, playful tone to it, something I certainly wasn't feeling in the slightest.

"You sure, because the whiskey comment was pretty…"

"Shitty?" I said, finishing his sentence.

"Yeah."

I shrugged. "Don't let it happen again."

Connor waited until Gabe returned to the house to say good-bye. While Gabe walked him out, I stayed behind, starting dinner, praying that moving back didn't turn out to be some huge mistake.

Connor

The sky was threatening rain as I drove down the long driveway to Gabe's place. The next time I'd drive down this driveway, my friend would be on his way overseas. I cut the engine of my truck and hopped out. Gabe sat on the front porch, beer in hand, with his feet up on the railing.

I chuckled as I made my way up the front steps. "I don't think I've seen you this relaxed in, well, forever."

Gabe laughed and tipped his beer bottle back, emptying the contents. "This is what you get when you're told to get out of the kitchen."

"I see." I glanced in through the screen door, seeing Cadence moving around the kitchen. "Is she cooking?"

Gabe nodded. "I fear she is." He chuckled.

"Cadence cooks?" I asked. "I figured she would have had this thing catered in."

"Nah, she became all domesticated when she lived with Grams." Gabe chuckled. "I seriously was afraid to eat when I first went out there, but her food is actually good."

"Don't think for one second I can't hear the two of you from in here!" Cadence yelled from inside the house.

I looked at my best friend and we both laughed. "Oh, Cadence, chill out!" Gabe yelled. "Do me a favour and bring us a beer."

"You've got legs. Get your own beer!" she yelled back.

"How about I get us another beer?" I questioned, making my way inside the house. When I stepped inside the kitchen, the smell of food caused my empty stomach to grumble.

"What's for dinner?" I questioned, sticking my head into the refrigerator and grabbing two bottles of beer from the door.

"Lasagna, garlic bread, and if you both behave your-self, devil's food chocolate cake for dessert," Cadence replied as she dropped a spoonful of icing on the cake.

"Sounds great," I said, dipping my finger into the bowl that contained the icing.

Cadence glared at me as I licked the frosting from my finger. "Really?"

I smiled, reached in again, and took another swipe at the sweet icing. I couldn't help myself as her eyes met mine. I brought my finger to her lips and gently touched them, leaving a smear of chocolate icing behind. I gave her a smile and then turned and made my way back toward the front door.

"Connor, that isn't behaving yourself!" she yelled.

"What the hell did you do?" Gabe questioned me as I passed him his beer.

I chuckled. "Nothing. Just taste tested the icing. You all packed up?"

"Yeah, just have one last load of things in the dryer," Gabe answered just as the front door opened and Cadence stepped out, holding a cooler in her hand.

"What you drinking there?" I questioned, reaching for the bottle.

"It's an iced pink lemonade," she said, holding the bottle up so I could see.

I reached out and grabbed it from her. Before she could protest, the bottle was already at my lips, and I'd taken a mouthful. The drink was very sweet and didn't mix well with beer at all. I began choking as it hit the back of my throat. I swallowed hard, cleared my throat, and handed it back to Cadence. "That is disgusting," I said, wiping my mouth with the back of my hand.

"I told her, but she still seems to be stuck back in her college days." Gabe chuckled.

"This is disgusting. Well, I have news: so is your spit all

over the bottle," she said, furiously wiping at the edge before taking another sip.

Cadence shook her head as she looked at the pair of us. "As for still being stuck in my college days, you both act the same damn way."

"You know, I remember when she used to love attention. Don't you?" I said, looking over at Gabe.

Gabe and I both burst out into laughter as Cadence stood there, speechless.

Cadence looked at both of us with disgust and then finally burst out laughing.

"Oh my gosh. She has a sense of humour," Gabe said, looking over at his sister.

"I'm actually laughing at the pair of you. You two idiots ready for dinner?"

"Starving," I said, holding the door open for her.

Gabe followed behind as we all made our way into the kitchen and sat down at the table. Cadence carried over the tray of lasagna and quickly slid the garlic bread into the oven, pulling it out only a few minutes later.

"Looks good," I said, watching as she carried over the plate of garlic bread and set it in the centre of the table. Gabe and I, as if on cue, reached at the same time and grabbed a piece from the plate.

"My god, it's like you are animals," Cadence grumbled as she sat down and helped herself to a piece of lasagna.

"Well, we work like them so..." Gabe grumbled. "God, I'm starving."

The table grew quiet as we all began eating. It was the best lasagna I'd tasted. I hated to say it, but Ella's lasagna couldn't even begin to touch this. Where the hell did Cadence learn to cook? Like I'd said, when I mentioned a meal to her, I figured she would have had it catered in from The Crispy Biscuit.

"This is fantastic, Cadence," I said between bites.

"Thanks," she muttered, taking a bite of bread.

"No, really, Cadence. It is," Gabe said, already having cleared his plate and going in for seconds.

"It's really nothing. Just an old recipe from Grams. I was afraid it wouldn't turn out. It's been a long time since I made it. I haven't really had anyone to cook for, for a long time."

I stretched in my chair, taking a minute to let the food I'd eaten settle before deciding if I wanted more.

"Don't say it's nothing. It's really good. You should cook for people more often," I said.

Cadence met my eyes, a sadness behind them I hadn't noticed until now. She said nothing, got up, and placed her plate in the sink before pulling down dessert plates along with mugs for coffee.

While Gabe finished up his plate, I took mine over to the sink as well and started helping to clear the table.

"What do you think you are doing?" Cadence asked.

"Clearing the table?" I answered, as I carried the tray of lasagna in my hand.

"Nope. Put that back. You are a guest."

"Oh please, I am not a guest. I practically live here." I chuckled, looking at Gabe for some sort of agreement, only he said nothing, because he knew better.

"I say you are a guest tonight. So, sit your ass back down in that chair."

I walked up behind her, placed my hand on her hip, and leaned into her ear. "You know, it's a real turn on when you get all bossy." I couldn't help but chuckle. I'd always loved it when Cadence tried to act all tough and tell us what to do. She was like that when she was younger, too. It was one thing I'd loved about her.

I watched as her cheeks heated at my comment. Then I looked over to see Gabe, still shoving food into his mouth. Cadence said nothing as she met my eyes, then surprised me by elbowing me right in the ribs.

I let out a groan and sat back down on my chair and met her eyes. "Don't," she mouthed so not to attract Gabe's attention.

"Who wants dessert?"

"Me," I said.

"Anyone else besides you?" She giggled, waiting for Gabe to say something.

He looked up from his plate, where he was sopping up

the sauce from his lasagna with his garlic bread and smiled. "Yes, please. I heard the icing is to die for."

"Oh lord help me."

We both chuckled as Cadence looked over at me and shook her head. She cut three pieces of cake and plated them, then poured three cups of coffee from the pot that had brewed, handing a mug and a slice of cake to each of us.

Once dinner was over, Gabe and I returned to the porch while Cadence cleaned up inside. "Hope you enjoyed dinner," Gabe said as we both sat down.

"Hard not to. I'm not really a cook so..."

"This is true."

"Hey..." I exclaimed.

"You said it, man."

I leaned back against the chair I'd sat down on and placed my hands behind my head. Tonight felt good. It felt normal. It hadn't felt that way for me in a very long time.

"I was watching you two tonight," Gabe said in a low voice.

"Uh-huh."

"For once, I don't think I need to worry about her. Or you."

I looked over at him, wondering what the hell he meant by that. "Why do you say that?" I questioned.

"Because for the first time in a year, I saw my old

friend return. And for the first time in five years, I saw a glimpse of my sister again."

I looked off into the distance. I didn't have a comment about that. The only thing I knew was that it felt good to let go, be in the moment, and not let the nightmare of losing Ella be in the forefront of my mind every single second.

Cadence

Rain pelted against my bedroom window. I rolled over in bed just as a loud crack of thunder shook the house. I glanced at the clock. It was almost three in the morning. I'd barely slept a wink. Connor had left relatively early last night, and Gabe and I had watched a little TV before we both said good night.

I rolled onto my side, trying to get comfortable. I was concerned for my brother, for his safety. It wasn't something I'd never felt before because I had when he was deployed the last time. I'd gotten used to it not being at the forefront of my mind. Now, it was back and in full force.

I let out a sigh and kicked off the covers. I wasn't used to the strange noises of this house any longer. When I'd come back for Ella's funeral, I'd stayed at the bed and breakfast in town. I'd planned to do the same now because I didn't want to stay in the house alone. I'd eventually asked Gabe what had happened, and he told me that Harry had suffered a fall and that Bessy had to close. Word in town was that they were going to put the place up for sale.

I sat up on the edge of the bed. There was no point in lying here if I couldn't sleep. I grabbed my sweater at the end of the bed and threw it around myself before quietly making my way downstairs. I went into the kitchen and had just sat down with a mug of coffee when I heard the stairs creak.

"What are you doing up at this hour?" Gabe asked sleepily. He shuffled into the kitchen, grabbed a mug and poured himself a coffee.

"I should ask you the same."

"Well, for starters, I'm not used to hearing footsteps in the house in the middle of the night." Gabe shrugged, sitting down across from me.

"I barely made any noise. Are you saying I woke you?"

"Let's just say you made enough noise. Plus, since you are taking me to the airport today, I thought I'd get up and take care of things around here so you don't have to when you get back here. So, no, it wasn't you that woke me."

I smiled. It was nice of him to think of me, but really, he didn't have to. "Thanks, but I'd get it done."

"I know, I just, I guess I just wanted to help. One last

run around the cattle barn before I leave." He shrugged. "I'm gonna miss them." His eyes dropped to his mug. I could tell something was on his mind. "Now, why are you up?" he asked, his voice low.

"Couldn't sleep. Strange house." I shrugged. Truth was it had nothing to do with the house. I'd grown up here. It was all the memories that had been running rampant through my mind since I'd returned.

"You sure that is it?" he asked, leaning back against his chair.

I didn't want to admit to my brother that I was worried about his safety. I didn't want him to make fun of me. "Are you worried about me?" he questioned.

I met his eyes. He knew. I couldn't let him know, so I shrugged.

"Ha, you are actually worried about me."

I blew out a breath. "Why does that seem so weird to you?" I asked. "I worried about you the last time you were gone, as well."

Gabe shook his head. "I know. I just figured that now, you'd be glad I was out of the way for a bit." He winked.

I frowned. I didn't know what that was supposed to mean. Why would I be glad that he was out of the way? "Gabe, I don't understand."

Gabe let out a deep breath and looked over at me. "I see the way you look at him. Don't think I don't."

I could feel my cheeks heat. "I...I..."

"Don't, Cadence. What I did when we were younger was wrong. I knew there were boys at school who liked you, but I also heard them all talk in the locker room. I didn't want you to become part of the rumor mill. As for Connor, I knew you liked him."

I looked at my brother. Was he confessing that fixing Connor and Ella up had been wrong? I reached down under the table and pinched the inside of my leg to make sure this wasn't some sort of dream I was having.

"He liked you too. He never said it, but I saw how he looked at you."

"You know, I just told you I was worried about your safety. Are you trying to make me regret saying that?" I questioned, trying hard to lighten this conversation.

"No, Cadence, that is not what I am doing at all. Remember when I beat up Paul Longshire in school?"

"Yeah. Dad was so pissed at you when his dad came to our house. I thought you were a goner." I laughed. "Why did you beat him up? Dad wouldn't tell me."

"I hit him because he said some things about you. Horrible things, and I was defending you because I didn't want the guys coming around you. Not guys like that."

I shrugged. "Okay. I don't see what that has to do with Connor."

"Connor had been there—for that fight. He'd tried to talk some sense into me, but I pushed him away and went on about how my friends would not take a turn with my sister. After that night, he started ignoring you, and he started asking me to fix him up with someone."

I got up from the table and took my mug back over to the coffeepot, filling it up. Then I reached into the fridge and added a generous amount of cream to the coffee before sitting back down.

"Say something," Gabe said, watching me.

"Gabe, I have nothing to say. I told you before I left the Midwest I wasn't coming back here to be his second choice. So, if that is some plan the pair of you have concocted, then I'll tell you right now, you better let him know not to bother trying."

Gabe blew out a breath and shook his head. "It's not something we've concocted. He needs someone. I'm all he has, and I'll be gone. He needs healing, and if anyone can heal him, it's you."

I took a sip of my over-creamed coffee. Why I'd added it I'd never know. I'd only ever drank my coffee black. It was almost as if I'd decided that punishing myself physically would be better than the mental punishment I'd been enduring for the last few years.

"And you are absolutely certain I am the right choice for the job?" I questioned.

"Of course you are the right choice! He hasn't smiled like that for a long time."

"Okay, because look at what happened to the last two

people I cared for," I said, sitting back against my chair. "They both died."

Gabe met my eyes and shook his head. Without another word, he got up from the table and left the room. Just when I thought he was gone, he stuck his head in the kitchen door. "Cadence, you are definitely the right person for the job. Gram and Gramps lived a good life, but they were old. It was their time. Enjoy your coffee. I have to get to work."

Connor

September

It had been three weeks since Gabe left and I'd yet to see Cadence. You'd have thought that in three weeks our paths would have crossed. I'd been going over to the farm daily after doing all of the chores on my ranch. Since I had yet to see her, today I'd decided to head over early. I wanted to talk to Cadence and find out what tasks she needed help with the most because, until now, I'd been a supervisor.

As I neared the house, I saw her black truck parked off to the side under the large willow tree beside the house, which meant she was home. I cut the engine and climbed out of the truck. The front door was open, and as I approached the house, the door opened, and Cadence stepped outside.

"What are you doing here so early?" she questioned, a sound of shock in her voice, an unimpressed look on her face. Wearing a pair of worn jeans, a thin white T-shirt, and a pink sweater over top, she stood there holding a bowl in her arm, a whisk in the other hand.

"I came by because I wanted to talk to you. It seems I've been more of a supervisor around here, and with the amount of work I need to do at my place, well, I don't have the time to play that role. So, I came to see what you really needed help with around here."

She stopped stirring the contents of the bowl and shifted her weight to her right foot. "I see. Didn't my brother give you one of his wondrous lists of tasks to complete?" She rolled her eyes.

I chuckled under my breath. He had done exactly that. However, every day I'd gotten here, his crew had completed the entire list of things he'd given me, and I had very little left to do.

"He did. It just seems that the guys are getting everything done. So, I'm wondering if perhaps he made a mistake and didn't give me the right list."

"I see. Well, since I'm not sure what he told you to do, I don't know if I can help."

"That's why I wanted to drop over. I can tell you what

it was he told me to do. I wanted to know if there were things you needed done or if I'm simply wasting my time coming over here every day. Since I haven't seen you since Gabe left, I figured I'd pop over this morning instead."

I wasn't an idiot. I knew she'd been avoiding me. She knew it too. I could tell from the look on her face when I said I felt like I was wasting my time.

"If that is how you feel, Connor, by all means...I'm more than capable of running this place," she bit out, still stirring whatever was in the bowl with vigor. "Despite what my brother thinks."

I chuckled. Most people would think Cadence was in a bad mood, but this was exactly how I remembered her. Grumpy because she felt people were doubting her, so sure of herself she'd never ask for help if she needed it.

"Well, Cadence, this will probably come as a shock to you, but I know you are more than capable of looking after this place. In fact, I even told Gabe that. But he insisted I be here. So, I'll start by telling you I'm not here because of you. I'm here because Gabe asked me to drop in. Now, if you don't tell me what you need done, then I guess I'll just be on my way."

I turned around and began walking toward my truck when I heard her mumble a string of curse words under her breath. I did everything in my power not to burst out laughing.

"Connor, wait. I'm sorry. I shouldn't be that way, not

to you. I know you are only here to help. Look, Gabe mentioned something about the back fence needing to be repaired. He wanted to get it done before he left, but it didn't happen. So, before I could let the cattle out into the field up front here, can you maybe look?"

I nodded, not sure why she'd reconsidered her position. Normally, she'd be ready to start a fight, and it had been coming. I could see it. One thing with Cadence, she always had been a spitfire. She'd also always been way more stubborn than she needed to be and could never accept help when it was offered. The fact that she asked me to do something for her made me wonder if perhaps she felt like she was in over her head looking after this place. But I wasn't about to ask her.

"Not a problem. I'll head out there now. It will probably take me a couple of hours. Will you be home when I get back?"

"Yep." She dropped the whisk back in the bowl, turned around, and disappeared back into the house.

I sat at the kitchen table Saturday morning, drinking a hot coffee and eating a piece of toast. I didn't feel like making breakfast this morning. Honestly, I'd barely made a meal for myself since the night before Gabe left. I hadn't realized how much I missed being around people for meals.

It had been one hell of a morning on the ranch. I'd gone out when the ranch hands arrived, and we rotated the cattle from one field to the next. Then I had a mountain of paperwork to do, which was why I was back in the house while I left the ranch hands to come up with a way to repair the barn.

"Fuck," I muttered under my breath as my hand hit my mug of coffee, spilling the contents all over the paperwork I'd just completed. Grabbing a cloth just as the phone rang, I dropped the cloth down onto the papers and grabbed the phone.

"Hello."

"Connor, how are you doing?" I heard Ella's mom's voice come over the phone.

I closed my eyes. Today wasn't the day for this call. I didn't need to be reminded that Ella had died, or that the anniversary of her death had just passed. I didn't need to hear a lot of things she'd said to me, and I didn't want a replay of them. "Good, good. How are you?"

"Doing as well as we can be. You know, given the time of year. What about you?"

"Doing okay. Keeping busy. Lots to do around here," I answered.

"How are you making out with the repairs?" she questioned.

I didn't have the heart to tell her that nothing had come of it. I never should have mentioned the issues with the bank prior to Ella passing away. Then the storm hit, and I'd needed to blow off steam. I'd vented to them during one of our dinners earlier this year. It had probably been a mistake, and I hadn't realized that until they asked me every time we spoke if I'd gotten the funds yet. Including at her funeral and every time thereafter.

"Good. Coming along nicely," I lied.

"Good, I'm glad to hear that. So, the bank could give you access to the cash?"

I clenched my jaw. "No."

"Well, my dear, they can now. Bill just got off the phone with the bank manager in Willow Valley. We have paid off your loans and we had them deposit another hundred thousand into your bank account. So, you should be good to do the repairs that are needed. I know Ella would be happy to know that the house and barn are going to be getting the repairs that are needed."

I didn't know what to say. Tears clouded my vision as the weight of what she'd just said hit me. "Paula, I...I can't accept that. That's a lot of money."

"It is. Bill and I talked it over. We sold the cottage on the lake. Now. I called because I wanted to confirm with you the dates we will come by for the holidays."

My heart sank. They'd sold their cottage. I swallowed hard.

"Now tell me, what dates?" Paula asked again.

They had come every single year when Ella and I had been married. After her death, they came to spend Christmas with me, so I wouldn't be alone. It had given me some comfort, and I knew it gave them some as well, but the truth was I needed to move on. It was time, but Bill and Paula only ever wanted to focus on the fact that she was gone.

"What dates are you looking at, Paula?" I said, patting the cloth, soaking up the coffee.

"We thought we would come in December this year, the fourteenth? Thought we'd spend some time with you closer to Christmas. That way, you aren't alone, and you don't need to reflect on the fact that she died alone."

Anger boiled inside of me. She'd called with a wonderful gift and then had to ruin it with her guilt inducing words. Every time we spoke, she had to get that in there somehow. It shouldn't even hurt me anymore, but it did.

"So, we will see you then."

"Sounds good. I've got to be going. Got to get back to work. Taking some cattle down to the auction in Cedar Landing today," I said, my jaw tight with irritation.

"Drive safe, and we will see you in a couple of months. We are looking forward to seeing what you do with the house and barn."

"Sounds good. See you then," I said, hanging up the phone.

I pulled back into Willow Valley shortly after five. It had been a long drive out to Cedar Landing where I'd unloaded the cattle and left them at the auction house. Once I was finished, I drove back home. I did a lot of thinking on that drive. Mainly about what Ella's parents had done for me. This would change many things for me. Not only would I be able to get the repairs done on both the house and barn before winter, but I'd be able to hire some more help and invest in some more cattle.

The other thing that weighed on my mind was Bill and Paula. I doubted if they would ever get over the fact Ella was gone. It seemed they both lived each and every day in a stage of mourning, not letting themselves focus on the present. In some ways, that made me worry because it felt as if they thought I too should never get over her. It made me worry about what would happen when I did, and I started dating again. What about if I got married again?

I tried to focus and calm my mind as I pulled onto the street that went out to my place. As I drove down the stone road, I realized that tonight I wanted something to take my mind off things. I didn't want to go home to a quiet house to focus on the fact that Ella's parents would be here in December. It had taken me all this time to accept the fact that she was gone and to be okay with what had happened. I knew that once they were here, we'd rehash everything that had happened all over again. Doing so would open up the old wounds, the ones where I blamed myself for not being there when it had happened. I'd regretted ever saying that to them, because I felt they too had been looking for someone to blame. So, I took my trailer back to the ranch, unhooked it, and then took off out to Gabe's—or Cadence's, now.

I pulled up in front of the house and climbed out of the truck. I could see the living room lights on and made my way to the front porch. I was just about to step onto the first step when a movement out by the barn caught my eye. I glanced over to see Cadence leading her horse, Ember, back to the paddock. For the first time since she'd been back, she finally had a look of peace on her face as she dealt with her horse. I walked up a way, leaned against the fence post, and watched from a distance.

Watching her tend to her horse was attractive to me. It was something Ella never did, work with the animals. In fact, I could count on one hand how many times she'd set foot inside the cattle barn. Cadence had grown up on a farm and had always been actively helping with animals.

"You know, if you're going to stand there and watch, you could come down here and give a girl a hand," she called out.

I chuckled to myself and made my way toward the paddock. "Well, I certainly wouldn't want to step on your toes. After all, you are completely capable," I said, resting my arms on the fence.

"That may be, however, she bucked me off on the ride."

One minute, I was leaning up against the fence, the next, I was right beside her, taking the saddle from her hands, placing it down on the ground. "Are you all right? Did you break anything?" I questioned, immediately putting my hands on her body, feeling around and watching for any sign of wincing or pain on her face.

"I'm fine, Connor. Just knocked the wind out of me, I guess. There was a bear off in the distance. I saw the bear first and was watching it instead of paying attention to Ember. I just didn't expect it."

"Yeah, but I mean, you are sure you're okay? A fall off a horse isn't something to take lightly. Did you hit your head?" I asked, bringing my hand to the back of her head.

She met my eyes and placed her hands on my chest. "I'm sure. Like I said, just had the wind knocked out of me."

"Where was this bear?" I asked, looking off in the direction she used to ride.

"Um, out in the far, far field."

"Close to here or not?"

Cadence shook her head, then looked down to where my hands were resting on her arms then up at me. "What are you doing out here this time of night?"

I slowly let my hands fall back to my side, and I carefully slid the reins from her hand. "Didn't want to be alone tonight. Too many demons up here." I pointed to my head. "So, I thought I'd come out here and see if there was any work to be done. Good thing I did. I'll take a trip out to the field on one of the other horses, check for the bear."

"I see." She let go of the reins and averted her eyes. "The bear took off while I was out there. I don't think we need to worry about it."

"I'll feel better if I look. First, I'll take care of Ember. Then I'll head out to the field and look while you go in and..." It was on my mind to tell her to take a hot bath, soak, and relax, but I bit my tongue. Cadence never liked being told what to do. As our eyes met, I could see a light blush on her cheeks.

"Get dinner?" she asked, meeting my eyes.

Dinner sounded great and, as if on cue, my stomach let out a growl.

"His stomach has spoken. Dinner it is!" Cadence let out a giggle and turned and made her way toward the house. It had been a giggle I hadn't heard in ages, but it was one I had heard and, at the moment, sounded like music to my ears. I watched her walk away, watching her hips sway back and forth. Ember stomped her foot and let out a huff. I chuckled. "All right, Ember, hint taken," I said, leading her to her stall in the barn and filling her water and feed buckets.

"That was excellent," I said, placing my fork down on the table and sitting back in the chair.

"Glad you enjoyed. Did you want any more?" she asked.

"Maybe just a little more." I chuckled and slid another small piece of bacon-wrapped chicken onto my plate. "I've not really been making too many meals for myself. Didn't realize how hungry I've been."

"You need to eat, Connor."

"I do, just not meals."

"Why not? You ate a meal tonight, and one with Gabe and I before he left. Do you really not cook?"

I looked at Cadence and shook my head. "No, I cook. I guess it's just difficult cooking for one all the time. Plus, most nights I'm exhausted."

Cadence nodded. I could see she knew full well what I

was saying. After all, she'd lived alone after both her grandparents were gone.

"I totally understand. It was harder for me after my grandparents were gone. If you'd like, since you are here in the afternoons, you are more than welcome to stay here for dinner. I'll cook, and that way I'll have some company too."

Did I hear her invite me for dinner every night? What was that about? Cadence hadn't exactly been friendly towards me in the past, especially once Ella and I had started dating. In fact, she had even pushed Ella away. The first time in years that she even acted a little like herself had been at the funeral. I blew out a breath and looked over to see she had rested her chin on her hand and looked at me awaiting my response. I wasn't sure how to answer her, but I was also tired of being alone and living in this screwed-up reality of mine.

"That would be good. I can keep an eye out for that bear, too. Don't want it getting up here too close to the cattle or horses." It was the best answer I could come up with. Besides, I didn't want her to think it was anything more than a pair of friends hanging out. I also didn't want her brother to kill me when he returned.

"So, then I guess you didn't find the bear?"

I shook my head. "No, but I saw signs. Other than that, the field was empty. So, for now if you take Ember out, stay out of that field."

"I can do that." She smirked.

"I mean it, Cadence, I'm not asking. Let me know if you see it again or see signs. A bear like that will kill those cattle out there." I wasn't kidding. A bear was a serious matter, not only for the cattle and horses, but being near to the house was dangerous as well.

"I will do as you ask," she said. "Now enough of all this serious talk. Please tell me, what would you like for dinner tomorrow night?"

Cadence

October

I walked down the main street in Willow Valley, taking in all the colours of the leaves that had changed. Red, yellow, and orange trees now lined the street, making for a beautiful display that mixed with the cooler morning air made it feel more fall-like than ever.

I'd stopped coming into town daily since that night in September when Connor had shown up unexpectedly. Since then, he'd spent every single evening with me. I'd spend my mornings doing farm chores, and then I'd spend my afternoons getting meals ready, then after dinner some nights, we'd play cards or watch a little TV together.

Today I had no choice but to come into town. I needed groceries, and since I was here, I decided I'd go in and pick up dinner from The Crispy Biscuit.

I walked up the street, taking my time checking out all the fall window displays each store had set up. The entire town was celebrating fall, the biggest celebration being held across the street at the fall fair. Kids yelled and screamed as bells rang out, signifying they'd won the game they were playing.

When I finally reached The Crispy Biscuit, I opened the door and stepped inside. The place was full, people from all over town, plus some outsiders who were seated inside sipping pumpkin spiced coffees while eating other pumpkin inspired goodies.

"Can I help you?"

"Yes, Cadence Bently. I'm here to pick up my order." I smiled at the young brunette behind the counter.

"Ah, yes. One moment. It's in the back."

I walked over to the display case and searched out what sorts of things they had for dessert when I spied a tray of pumpkin scones. I remembered they'd been Connor's favorite when we'd been younger.

"Can I get you anything else?"

"Two of the pumpkin scones, please," I answered.

Once I paid, I made my way back toward the door. That was when I spotted a flyer for the Christmas tree lighting. It was being held at the end of November. I smiled to myself. I hadn't been to the holiday tree lighting here in Willow Valley since I was in my teens. I could remember then it had been one of the town's signature events. I wondered if it had changed much. The last one I'd been to was the Christmas before Ella and Connor had gotten together. I made a mental note of the date and left the diner.

I got back to the farm a little after two and put dinner into the fridge. Connor had parked his truck beside mine, and I looked out toward the barn where I saw him working away with one of the farmhands. I made my way down to the barn where I saddled up Ember. I had just gotten on her when I heard Connor's voice behind me.

"Heading out for a ride?" he questioned, coming over to me.

"I am. Just going to go out to the small field and take a ride around. It's a beautiful day for a fall ride."

"Have you been out there recently?"

"No, I normally go out to the other field, but since that bear has been around, I haven't gone as you asked."

"Good. Well, be careful. I noticed a few gopher holes out there the other day. They need to be filled."

"No problem. I'll watch for them."

I clicked my tongue and Ember and I took off toward the field. After almost half an hour, I stopped to take in the view of the landscape. The trees out here were in full colour, bright and glimmering with the sun on them. I flicked the reins and guided Ember over to a side of the field we hadn't been in.

I was watching off in the distance as Ember trotted at a quick pace. Suddenly, I felt her fall from underneath me, and the next thing I knew, I was on the ground. I lay there for a minute, trying to catch my breath, and then slowly sat up. I looked over to where Ember lay. She hadn't gotten up and wasn't moving.

Panic filled me. She should have gotten up by now, I thought to myself. I pushed myself up off the ground, dusted off my pants, and ran over to her. I felt her legs, and the second I touched one of the front ones, she let out a cry. That was when I noticed the gopher holes, too many too count, just as Connor had warned. Tears clouded my eyes. I did not know how badly she had broken her leg, but there was no doubt in my mind that she had broken it. As I stood there petting my beloved horse, trying to figure out what to do, tears streamed down my face. "Hold on, Ember. Just hold on. I'll go get Connor."

I looked around, not sure if I should leave her or not, but didn't really have a choice. I didn't want her to be in pain. I took off in the direction we'd come, running as fast as I could. It was getting dark by the time I arrived back at the farm. I stopped at the gate to the paddock where I normally kept Ember and tried to catch my breath. My heart was beating wildly, my chest aching. Then I saw Connor come around from the barn.

I tried calling to him, but it did no good. My throat was dry, and I still hadn't caught my breath. It took me a minute, but finally I made my way over toward him, waving my arms. Finally, he caught me from the corner of his eye and stopped, then came running over to me.

"Cadence, what is it?" he asked, looking at me with worry.

"It's Ember. She fell," I cried.

I'd had Ember since I was a little girl. She meant the world to me. The hardest thing I ever had to do was leave her here when I'd moved to my grandparents'.

"In a hole?" Connor questioned. "Cadence, did she step in one of those holes?"

Tears rolled down my cheeks as I met Connor's eyes. I could see the worry and sadness lining his blue eyes. "Cadence, was it a gopher hole?"

I nodded my head, saying nothing. I knew the chances of her being able to be repaired were slim to none. I'd grown up with horses my entire life. I'd seen my share of them put down because of the holes out in the field. It happened all the time when my dad ran the ranch. All I could do was pray this wasn't the end for my Ember.

"Cadence, go call the vet. Tell him to meet me out there," Connor replied before taking off in the direction I'd come. "And whatever you do, don't come out into that field."

Darkness had fallen. Connor and the vet had been out there for two hours, closing in on three. I sat in the kitchen, a mug of coffee in front of me while dinner heated in the oven. The vet had arrived quickly, and I'd had one of the farmhands take him out to the field to meet Connor.

I was just about to get up and pour some more coffee into my mug when I heard the front door shut. I closed my eyes, sending one more prayer upstairs for my beloved horse, then pulled the casserole out of the oven.

"Dinner's ready. Just got the casserole heated through. Why don't you come on in and sit down?" I said, as if nothing were wrong.

I heard footsteps behind me and turned to see Connor standing in the doorway, hat in his large hands. I placed the casserole in the middle of the table, on the protective pads I'd placed down, then turned to grab a large spoon.

"I picked it up from The Crispy Biscuit. I hope you like broccoli and cheese casserole. I've not had this one before. Oh, and when I was in town, I stopped at the hardware store and pick up all the items you asked for to make those repairs."

I met Connor's eyes. Immediately, my throat got tight.

He didn't need to say anything; he didn't have to. I already knew that Ember was gone and that there was nothing he could have done to save her.

Immediately, I covered my mouth to stop the sobs that were trying to escape. I turned away from him, hiding my face, but my body betrayed me, shaking as the stifled sobs tried to escape. He wasted no time. He stepped across that kitchen floor and immediately wrapped his muscular arms around me. I turned toward him, his touch causing the dam to break and the tears to flow, and I buried my face in his chest.

Two weeks later, Connor and I sat on the front porch after dinner. I'd been struggling each day since we put Ember down. I'd pretended like everything was fine, but deep down inside, I was a mess, and I knew Connor knew it.

I sat down on the porch swing beside him. He patted the cushion right next to him and placed his arm across the back. I met his eyes and moved over, resting my head on his shoulder, as I adjusted the blanket I brought out up and around my shoulders.

"You've been quiet lately. You sure you're doing okay?"

I shrugged. "Not really, but I'm trying. I miss that damn horse so much," I said, tears welling up in my eyes.

"It gets easier." He wrapped his arm around me in a comforting embrace. "If you'd like, I can always bring Cinnamon over here. He loves to get out for a ride every now and again."

I blew out a breath and quickly wiped a tear from my eye. "Oh, I don't think so. Ember was my baby. To be honest, I don't think I want another horse."

Connor rubbed my arm, pulling me in closer to him. "I don't mean as a replacement. Just as a friend. I know how much you love getting out for rides."

"It's okay. No need. There's a lot of work to be done around here before winter," I said, sitting up and fixing the blanket again.

We both grew quiet as I curled into his side once again. This was how things had become between us. We enjoyed meals together, movies, occasionally we could talk, and then on the nights things were really bad, we'd comfort one another. I let out a deep breath, along with a sigh. "Thanks for the offer, though."

"Anytime you want me to bring him over, just ask. I can tell you, though, that life will go on and you will love another horse again. That I promise you."

"Really? Is that how it works?" I questioned, thinking

back to my conversation with my brother before he'd left. How he'd told me that Connor needed someone and that I could be that someone. That perhaps I could be the one to heal him. "Because that isn't how it looks from where I'm sitting."

I shifted nervously and sat up, pulling the blankets tighter around me. Connor looked over at me, a questioning look on his face.

"Why do I feel we aren't talking about horses?" he asked.

I hadn't meant for it to come out the way it had. It had irritated me that Connor just couldn't let the horse issue go. I looked at him and then stood up, walked over to the railing, and leaned against it, looking out over the fields.

"Cadence?"

I closed my eyes, steadying my breath, doing my best to keep from crying. Losing Ember had stung. He'd warned me, and yet I didn't listen. I never should have taken her out there. Yet I had to remember that it hadn't been Connor's fault, and here I was, taking it out on him.

"I'm sorry. I didn't mean to say it like that. It's just Gabe asked me to help you, and well, perhaps had he said those words I just said to you, then maybe you'd be dating someone right now," I answered, not hiding my thoughts from him.

Connor was silent for a long time. I felt horrible. I told

Gabe not to leave me in charge of this shit. I warned him that the last people I'd cared for ended up dead. I had a feeling my friendship, or whatever this was with Connor, was heading to the same place as my grandparents.

I leaned against the railing, listening as I heard Connor's footsteps on the old wooden porch. He should just leave. He wanted to leave. I knew he did. I could sense it. I was just about to turn to him and tell him to go when I felt his large hands on my shoulders.

He spun me around so I was facing him. I didn't look up. I didn't meet his eyes. I just kept my eyes trained on his chest. That was when I felt his finger on my chin. He tilted my head up, just until our eyes met, and that was when he leaned forward and placed his lips on mine.

He was hesitant. I could feel the tension in his body, in his lips. At first, I couldn't breathe. I could feel my body shaking, but the longer his lips were on mine, the more relaxed we both became. His lips danced over mine, and I could feel an overwhelming heat building in my body.

Then our lips parted, and I slowly opened my eyes, meeting his. "It only appears that way, Cadence, that life hasn't moved for me, because the girl I'm interested in hasn't taken notice of me just yet."

My cheeks were on fire as he looked into my eyes. He gently smiled as he cupped my cheek with his hand. "Hopefully, now I've given her enough of a hint, because lord knows the same feelings just rose from me as they did the last time I kissed her. I feel alive." He said nothing more, just made his way down the front steps of the porch. He was just about to his truck when he turned and returned partway.

"Cadence, I was wondering if you'd like to go to the fall fair with me tomorrow night? Tomorrow is the last night, and not only will there be fireworks, but dancing as well."

I softly smiled. I hadn't been to that fall fair since I was fifteen. Connor didn't dance then, not that I'd have had the courage to ask him. Instead, I'd danced with my brother. I slowly nodded my head. "I'd...I'd love that."

"Okay."

"Okay," I repeated, still feeling giddy at what had just transpired between us. Perhaps Gabe was right. Perhaps I was what Connor needed. Perhaps he was what I needed as well.

I heard the engine of his truck roar to life, and I watched as he took off down the driveway, leaving me alone with thoughts and memories of that kiss.

Connor

As I drove through town, that kiss was all I could think about. It had sparked something inside of me and, for the first time in months, I felt alive. I hoped she felt it too, because she was oblivious to the fact that I liked her. She never picked up on the brief glances I gave, or the long, lingering ones, but that was Cadence. I didn't know why I'd think she'd change now. She always had been that way, even when we were younger.

After I'd shoved that line of crap at her that even I didn't believe, it was her words that had woken me up. She'd been right, and I'd had to prove to myself the words I'd shoved at her about her situation were true for me as well. No one had ever taken the time to say those types of things to me, except for her at that moment. Her words had woken something inside of me, and I was thankful for that. She'd called me on my shit, in a roundabout way. Gabe used to do that, but regarding this situation, he hadn't. All he'd said to me was to take the time I'd need and eventually things would get back to normal. Whatever normal would look like for me, I didn't know.

Thinking about that kiss, how her soft lips felt against mine. When I'd asked her to the fair, I'd fully expected a no, but when I saw the colour of her heated cheeks and the look in her eyes, I somehow knew my ask would be accepted. I'd fallen into a restful sleep and, for the first night in a long time, I didn't seem to fight the same demons I'd fought every night since Ella had died.

That kiss also helped me realize that somewhere along the line, I'd gotten over Ella. I was ready for someone else, someone new. It was everyone else around me who hadn't, which was holding me back. Since they hadn't gotten over the fact Ella was gone, it was them who were keeping me where I was. That was what was making it hard for me to move on.

It was a little after four when I left the barbershop in Willow Valley. I wanted to clean myself up a little before heading out to Cadence's place to pick her up for the fair. It had been months since I'd had a proper haircut and a shave. I felt like a new man as I drove down the driveway toward her house.

Making my way over to the door, I gave a knock before walking in. I stopped in my tracks when she appeared in the doorway to the kitchen wearing a beautiful floral-print dress, white sweater, and cowboy boots.

"Wow..." I said under my breath as she stood before me, staring back. "You look...different." I did not mean it to be insulting. She looked stunning, but different from what I was used to seeing her in daily.

"Different? I should say the same thing about you. I barely recognize the man standing in front of me. In fact, it's been years since I've seen him."

I smiled. "I didn't mean it like it came out. You look beautiful. I'm just not used to seeing you in anything other than jeans and work clothes. Which doesn't look bad, it's just..."

"Same here." She softly smiled as our eyes met. At that moment, we exchanged unsaid words between us.

"You just about ready?"

"Just making us a couple of coffees to-go for the drive." She winked. "Figured you could use one."

I smiled. "A woman who knows the way to my heart," I muttered.

We stood off to the side, watching as residents of Willow Valley, young and old, danced around the floor. It seemed the entire town was out tonight. Bessy and Harry sat over in the corner, Harry in his wheelchair. Then there was Vi and Jed. They'd come all the way out from the retirement home. Some other residents sat with them watching the dancing.

"Hey, Connor, good to see you out," Trinity said, stepping up beside us. She waved over to Vi and Jed as I, too, lifted my hand, waving hello.

"Hey, Trinity. How's Thomas? Nice to see Vi and Jed came out." I stepped back and introduced Cadence. "Trinity, this is Cadence Bentley."

Cadence smiled. "Hello, nice to meet you."

"You as well. You must be Gabe's sister. I know you grew up around here. Vi over there used to run Bluebird Books. Now I run it."

"Yes. I used to come in there all the time before I moved." She nodded. "I used to love that store. I'll have to come by and pick up something to read soon."

"Would love to have you! Well, welcome back to Willow Valley. We had heard you were returning. Oh, and to answer your question, Connor, Thomas is here somewhere. He was wondering how you were doing with the ranch?"

"Things are coming along nicely." I nodded.

"Hey, Connor," a man said from behind us, and we both turned to see Thomas approach and hand Trinity a drink. "Nice to see you're out and about this year."

Thomas held his hand out for Cadence while introducing himself. "Miss, nice to meet you. I'm Thomas Jenkins. I own Jenkins Woodworks, and I'm attached to this here beauty," he said, pulling Trinity to his side.

"Ah, yes, I saw the sign beside Bluebird Books when I was in town the last time. Nice to meet you both."

"You as well. If you'll excuse us, we are going to dance. Trinity dragged me here."

Cadence and I both let out a laugh as Trinity rolled her eyes while pulling Thomas to the dance floor.

"Care to dance?" I asked, holding out my hand for her to take.

She slid her small hand into mine and we both took our time heading over to an empty spot on the floor. We were just about to start when the DJ stopped the music and a slow song began playing. We looked around the room as couples moved together and began slowly swaying to the music.

I could feel my heart in my throat as I met her eyes. I could tell she was just as uneasy as I was, and when I didn't pull her in, she pulled away, but I stopped her. Pulling her into my arms, we both stood there for a moment, looking into one another's eyes before we began swaying to the music.

As I held her in my arms, soon the others in the room fell away from us. With her in my arms, her head resting against my chest, I felt a sense of peace fall around me.

The feeling of holding her against me felt so right. It was when she lifted her head from my chest and looked into my eyes that I lowered my head and met her lips, just as the song stopped.

We'd danced the evening away, then left the dance floor to make our way over to the small pond in the park where they'd be setting off fireworks. Weaving through people and families that had set up in the park just off the main street of Willow Valley, we finally came to a clearing.

"Where did you want to grab a seat for the fireworks?" I asked, as we exited the midway where I'd just won Cadence a small stuffed pink bear.

Cadence carried the bear and a blanket over her arm for us to sit on. "Yes, where should we go?" she asked, looking at all the people who had grabbed a spot earlier in the evening, which was probably something we should have done.

We both scanned the park, looking for an empty spot and then pointed to an area over at the edge of the trees. "What about over there?" we said in unison, causing us both to laugh.

Making our way over to the area, I helped Cadence

spread the blanket out on the ground. We'd been sitting for about five minutes, listening to chatter all around us, when Cadence rubbed her arms.

"Who would have thought it would be this cold down here?"

"Used to warm October nights, are you?" I chuckled.

Cadence rolled her eyes and laughed. "No, but it seems colder tonight."

"Well, you can sit a little closer if you like," I said, patting the spot in front of me on the blanket. "I'll keep you warm. Then, once the fireworks are over, we can head over to The Crispy Biscuit and get some coffee. They are open late tonight because of the event."

Cadence thought for a moment. "Are you sure?"

"I wouldn't have offered if I weren't sure." I winked.

She hesitated a moment and then moved her way over toward me on the blanket. I leaned back, and she slipped in between my legs. At first she seemed stiff, not relaxed, and then finally, she relaxed against me. I wrapped my arms around her pulled her in close to me, breathing in the scent of her lavender shampoo. "Is that better?" I asked.

"Much," she whispered as she interlaced her fingers with mine, now fully relaxing against me.

We sat there, curled up together under the night sky, while fireworks exploded above us. In my mind, it couldn't have been a more perfect evening.

Cadence

A half-eaten piece of pumpkin pie sat on the table between us as we laughed at something Connor had said. It was nice; the diner was quiet, only a couple of tables were full, so it made me more comfortable knowing we didn't have prying eyes on us.

"So, you know all about my situation, but I know little about yours," Connor said.

I smiled. "What are you referring to?" I questioned, taking a forkful of pie.

"Well, I know you went to help your grandparents, but tell me. Was there anyone in your life? A significant other?" He sat across from me, a serious look on his face.

"Are you asking if you may get beaten up tomorrow morning?" I laughed.

"Perhaps?" He shrugged, sipping on his pumpkin spiced coffee.

"You don't need to worry." I winked. "There isn't anyone."

"Cadence, you can't tell me you've been single this entire time. There had to be someone?" he asked.

I let out a breath; he was right, there had been someone. He was just someone I didn't want to think of anymore, or ever again. I nodded. "There was. A someone."

"And...?" He gave me a playful look. "Tell me more."

I buried my face in my hands at the memory of Daniel Oliver. He'd differed from any other man that I'd ever been attracted to. He was the assistant bank manager where my grandparents had done their banking. A suit, as some of my friends had called him. The girls I'd hung around with had warned me about him, yet I hadn't been able to see anything wrong with him.

"His name was Daniel Oliver."

"No offense but he already sounds like some stuck-up asshole." Connor chuckled.

I smiled. He'd hit that right, and yet he'd never even seen him. I nodded. "Yeah, you pegged him, and you've never met him."

"So what happened?"

"Well, I met him one afternoon when I'd stopped at the local bank to do some banking for my grandparents. I had to be granted permissions on their accounts and I had to meet with him. Of course, he was charming, good looking, and by the end of the appointment he'd asked me out."

"That's ballsy," Connor said, taking another bite of the pie.

"Yeah, it was, but I was young and naïve," I said, swiping some of the pumpkin filling with my fork.

"Uh-oh. This doesn't sound good," Connor replied, watching as I sucked the filling off my fork.

"Oh, well, it started out fine. I mean, we dated. He seemed to get along well with my grandparents at first. Then Grandpa took ill. Of course, my focus had to change, so my attention couldn't be on him every single second. I spent a lot of my time at the farm and with him at the hospital. Daniel really didn't like that. After Grandpa passed, and my attention turned back to him, he seemed okay again. We'd double date with my friend Olivia and her boyfriend, and things seemed to go really well. Then Grams came down with dementia."

"Let me guess, he got all bent again?"

"Yes, he'd want to do these things, but I couldn't just leave Grams alone. She'd just lost Gramps, and she'd been forgetting a lot of things. Some days she was fine, others not so much, and I worried about her constantly when I wasn't home. Daniel would make me feel bad about not being able to go out with him."

"You were taking care of family. He shouldn't get like that."

"True, but then a real man would understand that. Anyway, once I got some help from a couple of neighbours and could have some sort of life again, he was fine. Things went back to normal, and he'd be more forgiving if I wasn't able to come out. However, one evening Grams got violent with the ladies who were staying with her, and I had to rush away to head back home. That was when things turned worse. Daniel and I began fighting nonstop. One afternoon, Olivia called me while Grams was at a medical appointment. She said she'd seen Daniel out with someone else for lunch, a woman, and they appeared to be more than just colleagues or friends."

"He was cheating on you?"

"Yeah. At this point Grams was bad, and I just couldn't deal with any more of his nonsense. I knew where my focus needed to be, and it wasn't on a man who was behaving like a two-year-old and sleeping with someone else. So, a week later, when one of the home care nurses was at the house to see Grams, I ran to the grocery store. While I was gone, I figured I'd slip into the bank, have a word with Daniel, and be done with it all."

"Good, he deserved to be told. So what happened?"

"Oh, let's just say hell froze when I got to his office door."

Connor looked at me, concern lining his face. "What is that supposed to mean?"

"It means that I found out who the woman Olivia warned me about was."

"Let me guess, it was the neighbour chick who had been helping you with watching your grams."

I laughed. "Somehow, that would have been easier, but no. It was Olivia. My best friend."

Connor's shocked look made me giggle. "What? You mean she ratted on herself to you? That doesn't make sense."

"Yep, I opened the door to find Olivia plastered against the wall. My best friend with this...this suit, as she called him. Daniel was a very busy man at that moment with his hands full of her boobs. Right there, in the bank."

"Oh my..."

"Yeah, so the pair of them got told. Daniel begged me not to leave him...and Olivia, well, soon after I found them together, she found him with another woman in the same position. Daniel soon got fired from the bank, and Olivia still calls me every now and again. I think the guilt of what she did got to her."

"So you've heard from her since you moved back here?"

"Not yet, but she called right before I left. She even had the nerve to attend my grandmother's funeral. To be honest, I wasn't angry at her. I didn't even care because of the timing of it all, but I certainly wouldn't be friends with her again. Not when she consciously went after Daniel. I could never trust her again."

Connor grew quiet. "Is that why you and Ella went your separate ways?"

I avoided Connor's eyes. "No. We just grew apart," I lied, knowing full well seeing her accept a kiss from him, when she knew full well I'd planned to make a move on him, had nearly killed me when we'd been in our teens. "Plus, after I moved, it was harder to keep up with the day-to-day. Our lives just went in different directions."

The last part was truthful. However, knowing that my best friend in the entire world had stolen the boy I'd liked had truthfully broken my heart. Connor, of course, did not know I'd ever liked him, nor had Gabe. I was sure in Gabe's mind he was only doing what he thought was best to help his friend. Still, Ella had, and knowing she knew, and still accepted his advances, his proposal, it had made it difficult for me to fully forgive her.

"That's understandable. You were off dealing with your grandparents. Ella wouldn't have understood. I know she always wondered why you never called. She always wanted to be a shoulder for you. I'd tell her it was because you were probably busy and, of course, Gabe always filled us in on how you were, so it wasn't like we didn't get updates. I just remember so many times, her crying thinking you were angry with her. When I'd ask, she'd never tell me why, of course. I just chalked it up to pregnancy hormones." Connor chuckled.

"Did she ever talk to her parents about her and I?" I questioned, wondering if perhaps they'd mentioned something to Connor after they'd seen me at the funeral.

"I don't know." Connor shrugged. "Her parents and I don't view things the same way. I don't ask questions because I don't want to hear a lecture. Besides, they only call or come out twice a year. They claim it's too hard on them to be in what was once her house."

"Really? That's it. That doesn't sound like Mr. and Mrs. Connor."

"Clearly you don't know Bill and Paula very well. They are very good at making one feel guilty."

I looked at Connor, not sure what he meant by that comment. I wasn't sure I wanted to know because it sounded awful. Were they really blaming him for her death? I knew her parents well. They'd never made me feel that way in my entire life. "Care to elaborate?"

"Well, let's see. Days after Ella died, all I'd heard was that had I of been in the house, things probably would have been different. That I'd have been able to save her. They'd repeatedly said that at her funeral, not sure if you heard that. That went on for weeks. Paula would call up and have crying fits on the phone with me, blaming me."

"Connor, I did not know," I said, bringing my hand to

my heart. It hurt me to know that they had treated him like that.

"Each time they call, it's always close to the anniversary of her death. They called me six months after, then on the anniversary of her death. They'd started asking me if I were seeing someone, like it would be so bad if I was. Almost making me feel that I'd be cheating on her. It's almost as if they want me to stay single, blaming myself for her dying. It's almost like they don't want me to move on."

"That doesn't sound like either of them."

"It may not to you, but just trust me. It is."

We both grew quiet as we sat in the small booth. I looked over at him to see his eyes focused down on the table. I could see the hurt on his face, and I could only imagine the hurt going on inside of him. "Connor?" I said, reaching across and placing my hand on his. "You have a right to be happy. Screw what they think."

He looked up and met my eyes. "You are the first person to say that to me. Of course, you are the first person I told this to. I never mentioned it to Gabe."

"I mean it, Connor. It's probably a good thing you didn't mention it to him. He'd lose his temper." I giggled.

We sat there staring at one another. I wished he'd hold me in his arms again and kiss me like he had on that dance floor tonight. I wished I could be the one to make him happy, the way he should be. Regardless of what he felt, others thought. I also knew and was preparing myself because I feared perhaps I was the girl he was trying things out on. After all, we'd known each other for years and I was someone he was comfortable with. I feared how devastated I'd be if that were the case, if after he tried these things on me, I'd have to watch him do it with another woman.

"You know, Cadence, nothing has made me happier than I was tonight. Getting to hold you in my arms, dancing on that dance floor."

A feeling of warmth flooded my body. "I felt the same way," I said, my voice low as I slid my hand into his.

The drive back to the farm was a quiet one. Connor drove back, his hand in mine as we listened to some music. When we got back to the house, he walked me to the front door where we now stood, listening to the sounds of crickets and cicadas.

"Thank you for a wonderful evening, Connor," I said as I slid the key into the lock and pushed the inside door open far enough that I could turn on one of the living room lights.

"No, thank you," he said, leaning in and placing a kiss on my cheek.

As he pulled away, I went to say something, but he stopped me. "Cadence, I have something I want to say."

I could tell from his expression that it was important, so I waited while he gathered his thoughts.

"Remember how you said tonight that I deserve to be happy?"

I nodded. "Yes. It's the truth." It was the truth in my mind.

Connor cleared his throat. "Can I tell you something?"

"Of course."

"Gosh, I don't even..." Connor stepped away from me and shoved his hands in his pockets as he looked out toward his truck. Then he pulled his hands from his pockets and ran them through his hair. "Cadence, ever since I saw you again, it has reminded me of our teen years. I said nothing, well, because of Gabe, but..."

I closed my eyes. Was he going to say what I thought he was going to say? My heart beat faster as I stood waiting for him to continue. I feared if I said anything that he'd stop speaking and leave.

"Gosh,...I always liked you. Gabe was the one who hated when his friends said anything regarding you."

I frowned. "You...you...liked me then? Like back in

school, then?" I could hear the surprise in my voice and felt the shock of his words in my body.

He turned toward me and nodded his head. "Don't think I'm a bad man, Cadence, but Gabe set me up with Ella because I'd been complaining to him. I wanted a girlfriend, but not just any girlfriend, it was you I wanted. I just didn't know how to tell him. I'd seen how he handled those situations, and I didn't want it to be me on the ground being beaten by your brother. His friendship meant so much to me."

Tears stung my eyes at his honesty. Had he really sacrificed what he'd wanted because of his friendship with my brother? Had he only taken Ella as a second resort?

I cleared my throat. "Did you...did you even like Ella? Were you in love with her?" I questioned.

Connor turned away from me and once again focused his attention out into the darkness. I waited for his answer; I didn't want to push. Hell, I wasn't even sure I wanted to know the answer, fearful that she had lived thinking he loved her when he hadn't. I wished he would face me, so I could see his reaction, so I could read his expression, but he didn't.

"Not really, not at first. It was really you I wanted. I just... I settled. For a long time, I'd just pretend it was you. I know it was wrong. Once I got to know her, of course, I fell in love with her, but it wasn't like I imagined it would have been with you."

"Why didn't you ever say anything to me?"

Connor chuckled. "I never thought you were interested in me. Hell, I was a farm boy. Everyone in town hated my father. Most kids hated me because of his business dealings."

"That's not true."

Connor turned and looked at me. "It isn't?"

"No, it's not. I never hated you."

"You didn't?"

I didn't waste a moment; I gathered up every ounce of courage I had inside of me and stepped across the front porch, placed my hands on his cheeks, and kissed him. I knew it surprised him, but soon his arms wrapped around me and he was kissing me back. When we parted, I looked up at him.

"I never hated you. I liked you way more than you ever knew, and I kept it hidden well. Almost as well as I've kept it hidden from you now."

Instantly, his lips were on mine in a consuming kiss. Minutes later, completely breathless, he stepped away from me and, with one more kiss on the lips, he bid me good night.

Connor

Humming to myself, I checked on the new lot of calves that had been born a month ago. I'd slept so well last night, I'd gotten up early to come out and spend some time checking each one of them over. I'd just finished dumping feed and filling their water buckets when Joe came walking into the barn.

"Hey, Connor. Did you know there is someone up at the house?" he asked.

I frowned. "No."

"Yep, lights are on in the kitchen and there is a truck parked out front beside yours."

"What colour truck?" I asked, praying he didn't see a silver one. That would mean that Paula and Bill were here, and after the night I'd shared with Cadence, I wasn't in the mood for them.

"Looks like Gabe's truck, to be honest," Joe answered.

I smiled, excited at the thought that Cadence had finally come over. "All right. Care to take over here while I check it out?" I asked.

"No problem. Then once the others get here, we will finish up repairs on that fence and then we will start on the door to that barn. Should be able to get it finished by tonight so we can begin moving the cattle up to the front pasture."

"Sounds good. Oh, and the material for the feed barn will be here next week. It would be good to get on that right away."

"Not a problem," Joe said, taking over where I left off.

I made my way up to the house, an extra spring in my step, excited to see Cadence after last night.

I walked up toward the back door of the house and immediately stopped in my tracks at the smell of bacon. My stomach turned and my mind flashed to the day I'd found Ella. It took me a minute to compose myself, to fight the nausea I was feeling.

I climbed the back steps and stepped in through the back door. Cadence stood at the counter, chopping up onions while a pan on the stove containing the bacon cooked away.

"What is going on?" I asked abruptly.

Cadence turned around and smiled. "Oh gosh, I

wanted to surprise you with breakfast. I didn't figure you'd be back up at the house yet. Dammit," she said, wiping her hands on the apron she wore before grabbing a fork and flipping the bacon. "It was supposed to be a surprise."

My stomach was spinning as I watched her flip the greasy bacon strips in the pan. When I couldn't stand the smell any longer, I headed back out the back door and sat down on the steps. I couldn't be in there with that smell... that godawful smell.

A few minutes later, I heard the door open behind me and Cadence sat down next to me. Sliding her arm through mine, she leaned against my shoulder.

"Connor, did I... did I do something wrong?" she asked, her voice quiet.

I said nothing for fear I'd throw up before I got the words out. I took a moment, taking a few deep breaths, and then I looked over at her. "Nothing that you'd know about." It was true. She hadn't known the gritty details of that morning. Gabe had been the only living being I'd told, and I'd asked him not to say a word.

Cadence frowned. "Care to explain? I didn't mean to upset you."

I didn't want to remember that horrifying day, but I knew it was important for her to know. "I don't eat bacon anymore."

She looked at me, shock lining her face. "What? Who

the hell doesn't eat bacon? Gabe told me you guys used to eat it all the time."

"The keywords in that sentence are used to." I winked, leaning against her.

I could tell Cadence was confused. Hell, I was confused, and yet I knew the reason I didn't eat it. I looked away. I didn't want to go down that path, but knew I had to. "Cadence, the day that Ella..."

I felt Cadence place her hand on me and squeeze my arm, waiting for me to continue.

"The day Ella died, she'd been cooking breakfast. She'd collapsed in the pantry, and when I'd come in, bacon was still on the stove. Of course, it was burnt, but ever since I haven't been able to stand the smell of it. It reminds me of finding her, laying on the floor, her eyes wide, staring into nothing," I said as I nervously twisted the wedding ring that still sat on my finger.

Cadence said nothing. She just gripped my arm a little tighter.

"You know, no matter what I do, I can still see her laying there. I can still smell that burning bacon every once in a while, when I step into the house. When I came up to the house and smelled it, my fear was that I was going to walk in and find you in the same..." I closed my eyes, not wanting to say those words.

Cadence leaned against me and rested her head on my

shoulder. "I understand, Connor. Know that I'm not in the same position. I'm here and very much alive."

"I know," I whispered, interlocking my fingers with hers. "I just wish that someone else would understand and know what this feels like. So I know I'm not alone."

"You aren't alone, Connor," she answered, her voice changing tones.

"I'm not?" I questioned, looking at her.

"No."

I looked at her, at the sadness in her eyes as they fell away from mine. She ran her fingers through her hair, moving a loose strand behind her ear before meeting my eyes again. "Did Gabe tell you about our grandfather?"

I thought for a moment before shaking my head. "I don't think so."

"Gramps loved vanilla ice cream. Every Friday night he'd have some. One thing, it had to be homemade. He claimed the store-bought stuff didn't have enough vanilla flavour. Grams would make sure that there was always fresh cream for it, along with either vanilla beans or real vanilla extract. Friday afternoons, I'd make it. He especially looked forward to it after his cancer treatments had started. It was the one thing he looked forward to each week."

She smiled as she thought about the memory. She'd always had a pretty smile, but somehow, with the early-morning light shining on her face, she looked even prettier.

"Well, this particular Friday I'd forgotten to do a couple of things out in the barn. So, after we'd eaten dinner, Gramps ran out to the barn while I scooped out ice cream for the three of us. I had put in a little too much vanilla. It was all I could smell as I scooped the stuff into the bowls."

I could see that the memories were painful for her as they came flooding back into her mind. Her eyes were glassy, and she held a lot of tension in her shoulders.

"Anyway, I'd scooped out the ice cream and put the bowls on the table, then Grams and I sat down. Grams appeared to be a little worried, since Gramps had been gone much longer than he should have. I told her I'd head out to see what was up, but she insisted. So, off she went. Moments later, I heard her scream, and I ran out to the barn to find him unresponsive on the floor of the barn."

Cadence wiped her eyes as a tear spilled down her cheek. I went to pull her against me, but she fought me. Instead of allowing me to comfort her, she stood up and paced back and forth in front of me.

"Gramps passed away in the hospital four hours later. It was heartbreaking, and when we'd come home, the entire—and I mean entire—house smelled of vanilla. I cleaned up the three bowls of melted vanilla ice cream, which really wasn't that bad, but the smell of vanilla was awful, and it turned my stomach. It smelled that way for days and for the longest time after he'd passed, the thought of eating vanilla ice cream was appalling. I couldn't even use it in recipes for baking. Months passed, and one day, I came in from doing some work in the barn. It was shortly after they diagnosed Grams with dementia. I found her in the kitchen with the ice cream maker out. It was a Friday, and she'd made ice cream. The entire kitchen smelled of vanilla. While I fought the feeling of being sick, all she did was look at me, smile, and tell me how excited Gramps would be to have ice cream tonight after his treatment."

"Wow, Cadence, I did not know," I muttered.

"Gramps had been gone for almost a year, and here she was making ice cream as if he was going to be walking through the front door any minute."

"What happened?"

I watched her as she smiled at me and then let out a tight laugh. "Well...after dinner, we sat down and ate that ice cream. I had to choke it down. I had no other choice. I knew if I didn't, it would have crushed her."

"So even though it made you sick, you ate it anyway."

Cadence nodded her head and softly smiled. "When I looked at her, at how happy she was as we sat there, each of us eating this ice cream, it made it worth it. I'd not seen her smile like that in almost a year. The sad part was she'd set out a bowl for my grandfather. Only it just sat there waiting for a man who wasn't ever going to come. It was heartbreaking in some ways and beautiful in others."

"Didn't she wonder where your grandfather was?" I questioned, looking over at Cadence as her eyes welled with tears.

"Nope." She shook her head, a lone tear sliding down her cheek. "Never even asked. It became a common occurrence. Some nights she was sure he'd be home soon, and she'd worry for hours, while other nights she never mentioned him, even though the bowl would sit there. Not that long after, she'd forgotten most everything, and soon she barely knew who she was."

"Wow. I did not know."

"Of course not. How would you?"

I watched as she paced back and forth for a couple more minutes before I stood up and took hold of both her hands. She looked up at me and then wrapped her arms around me, resting her head against my chest, and sobbed while I held her.

Connor

Mid-November

Icy wind blew, making the tiny snowflakes that floated through the air appear to be dancing. We made our way down the main street to the park that only a few short weeks ago held the fall fair. She shivered.

"Hold on a second," I said, turning to stand in front of her. I adjusted her scarf, raising it over her red cheeks, and then raised the zipper of her jacket, pulling the hood up over her hat. "That better?"

"Much. Thank you."

I reached over and slid my gloved hand into hers as we

continued to walk. We took our time, stopping to look in at each of the shop's decorated windows.

Cadence and I had been spending more time together since Ember had to be put down. She'd finally allowed me to bring Cinnamon over, and she'd been out riding him daily. We'd been spending much more time together. Not only evenings for dinners, but she'd sometimes come and surprise me with breakfast or lunch as well. Some evenings we spent curled up together on her couch, watching a movie or TV show. Last night had been the first night we'd fallen asleep together while watching TV, and when I woke, she insisted I just stay the night on the couch.

I gave her arm a gentle pull as we crossed the street and made our way into the park. We stopped at a small table where Brooke and Tristan were handing out hot chocolate to anyone who wanted one.

"Thanks, guys. Smells great," I said, as she set the steaming cups down on the table.

"No problem. It's a newer recipe from last year. People say they like it better."

"Can't wait to try it. Are you taking a donation this year?" I questioned, knowing that they normally raised money for a local cause.

"We aren't asking, since they are here, but we are taking donations for Harry and Bessy."

I reached into my pocket and slipped a bill into

Brooke's hand. "There you go." I winked, as I grabbed two cups and handed one to Cadence.

"Thanks, Connor. You guys enjoy the evening." Brooke smiled and waved, then turned toward the next couple in line.

I handed Cadence her cup of hot chocolate, and we made our way over to an open space in the park.

"Thanks," she said, taking a sip. "Sure is colder than I expected."

I nodded. "Glad I told you to bundle up. I was cold out in the barn today, and that was without this wind." I looked at her again and noticed she was shivering. "You all right?" I questioned, worried that she was going to be too cold.

"Can you hold this for a minute?" Cadence handed me her cup, then undid her coat, slipping out of it quickly so she could adjust the shawl she'd been wearing to come up around her neck a little more. Then she quickly slid back into her coat and took her cup back from me.

Once our cups were empty, I carried them over to the trash can and made my way back over to her just as the music played. Within minutes, she shivered again, so I pulled her over to an empty picnic table and sat down, straddling the seat. I patted the bench, and when she sat down, I wrapped my arms around her in a protective embrace.

"That better?" I asked, my voice low.

She nodded her head, and together we watched as Mindy lit up all the trees in the park. The last one was the large one that had come from her farm for this year's Christmas. Everyone clapped and then sang "Silent Night," just like they'd done every year since we were kids.

I pulled her in closer just as we heard a throat clear behind us. "Two events in a row," we heard a familiar voice say and turned to see Thomas standing with Trinity.

"Hey, Thomas. Good to see you," I said, holding my hand out to shake his.

"It's good to see you out and about, Connor," Trinity said, giving us both a soft smile.

"Good to be out," I replied. It wasn't a lie. It felt good to get out with people again. It felt good to have a woman in my arms again.

"We are glad to see you back out. Trinity and I were getting very worried about you," Thomas said as he looked at me. "How's Gabe?"

It was just then that another couple came up beside Thomas and Trinity, both smiling our way.

"Oh, this is Ethan and Peggy," Trinity replied, introducing them to Cadence. "Peggy owns Peggy's Petals, the flower shop."

"Oh, yes, I drove by it when I came into town. And my brother is doing well. He's hoping to come home for Christmas but wasn't sure if he'd be able to the last I spoke to him."

"Ethan used to be in the military," I added. "You have him to thank for Gabe leaving," I said, closer to her ear.

"Nice to meet you," Cadence said, nodding toward Ethan.

"You guys gonna take a spin on the pond together? The four of us are heading over there now," Ethan said, taking hold of Peggy's hand. "I haven't skated in ages, so this might be worth the view." He laughed.

Cadence looked up at me, but I shook my head. "Nah, we were gonna go over and grab a coffee, do a little shopping, and then make our way back to the farm."

"Well, enjoy."

We watched as the four of them made their way over to the small pond that was now safely frozen for skating thanks to the cold snap we'd had the last two weeks. I looked down at Cadence, who pulled her hands inside her jacket sleeves and shivered again.

"Did you want to head back?"

She looked up at me, her eyes full of innocence, and nodded. "I'm sorry, I'm freezing."

"No sorry needed." I winked. "Let's go. We'll stop and grab a hot drink before making the drive back."

We stopped in at The Crispy Biscuit and placed an order for two cups of coffee to go. While we stood there waiting, Cadence leaned into me and asked if we could wait out front so we could continue talking quietly amongst ourselves. We had just stepped out the front door of the place when we noticed a bunch of young kids across the street. They started yelling something about kissing and mistletoe as they pointed in our direction.

I did my best to ignore them when I felt Cadence grip my coat and lift her gaze up. I looked up and noticed that we were standing right under the mistletoe that Brooke and Tristan hung outside to catch couples underneath.

"Hey, mister, aren't you going to kiss her?" one of the young kids shouted.

I looked at Cadence, whose cheeks were red, probably more so from the kid calling us out in public than the cold.

"Yeah, mister..." another young kid added. "Kiss her, kiss her."

I couldn't help but chuckle as the boy's mother grabbed the pair of them by the jackets and pulled them away. I pulled Cadence against me, warming her, when the door opened and Melinda stepped out just far enough to hand us our coffees.

"Have a good night," she sang as she went back inside.

I'd just handed Cadence her coffee when Brooke came over carrying the thermos that had been filled with hot chocolate and smiled at us both. "You two realize you are standing right under that mistletoe there..." She winked before she opened the door to the diner.

"Oh my god, I'm ready to die," Cadence mumbled as

more townsfolk looked our way with smiles on their faces, waiting for us to kiss.

I was about to grab her and meet her lips when we heard the cackle of a laugh I'd know anywhere. I turned to see Ella's Aunt LuAnn approaching us. LuAnn and I never got along. She barely got along with Ella. Most people in Willow Valley were afraid of her, and she loved to torment the children at events like Halloween.

Cadence leaned into me. "She's always hated me, Connor. We should just go." She whispered as she tugged gently on my hand.

Instead of listening, I ignored her and turned to face LuAnn. I wasn't afraid of her. We'd done nothing, but I knew LuAnn loved to stir the pot.

"Well, well, what's this we have here? Connor Darling, my sister-in-law's precious, widowed son-in-law, with his dead wife's best friend. Cadence, isn't it? Whatever are you doing back in town? Whatever would my sister Paula say about this?" she said, sauntering over toward us.

I turned my body toward LuAnn and was about to say something to her when Cadence tugged on my arm again.

"It's not worth it, Connor. Come on, let's go."

"Listen to her, Connor. It's not worth it. I already know the truth. That there was something going on between the two of you. I mean, you're always out at the Bentley farm since Gabe left. I've been watching."

Of course, she'd been watching. She worked for the Willow Valley Gazette as their head reporter. I was sure this would make a wonderful story for her to write up. The same way she wrote about me after Ella died. She'd deny it forever, but there wasn't a doubt in my mind that it was she who had written the incredibly hurtful article. She'd tried to say Ella had been the victim of an unfortunate accident and that I'd been the instigator of it.

I could feel Cadence play with my wedding ring I still wore, and when I looked down and back up toward LuAnn, she too had noticed.

"Out with her best friend, but yet still wearing the wedding ring, I see? I'll make a note of that for my article. I can see the headline now. "Poor Widow, Still Wearing Ring, but Dating Again." she said, waving her hands through the air as she appeared to imagine the article title already written in the paper. "Or wait, perhaps, Best Friend Steals Her Dead Best Friend's Husband. That has a better ring to it," she said, looking at me. "Oh, isn't that funny...ring to it." She laughed.

Anger boiled through me as LuAnn stood there, still laughing away. I was just about to respond when I felt Cadence pull away. She threw her coffee cup down on the ground and bolted from my side.

"Cadence!" I called, but it did little good. She ran toward the direction of where we'd parked the truck. I glared at LuAnn, ready to fight her, but decided it wasn't worth my time. We had done nothing. Instead, I took off after the person who was more important to me.

I finally slowed my pace as I caught up to Cadence. She faced the truck, standing against the door, and when I turned her around, she had tears streaming down her face.

I'd tried to talk to Cadence all the way back to her place, but she wouldn't even acknowledge me. I'd planned to just let her cool off and hoped we'd talk once we were back, but she had other ideas. Instead of waiting for me, she bolted from the truck before I'd barely come to a stop. She ran up the front steps, opened the door, and slammed it shut. I waited a moment, but when the inside lights didn't go on, I pulled away and made my way home. It was time to give Cadence some space.

Once home, I'd had half a mind to call Bill and Paula and tell them about tonight. LuAnn had zero rights to attack either of us the way she did. They needed to know about it, but once I thought of Cadence crying her eyes out, I didn't. Instead, I crawled into bed and stared at the ceiling for hours.

It didn't surprise me that Cadence didn't show up or call the next day. I didn't make a move to go to her place either. Instead, I worked on the ranch, and once I was finished, I hopped in the shower and got dressed for tonight. Cadence and I were supposed to make our way into town tonight to get her a Christmas tree. She'd even convinced me to get a tree. The idea at first sounded silly, but the more she spoke about it, the more it grew on me. It would be nice to feel the feelings associated with Christmas again. I just hoped that she'd gotten over last night and wanted to go, because I was looking forward to it.

I stood in front of the mirror, a towel wrapped around my waist, and ran my hand over my face, my wedding ring catching my attention. I looked down at my large hand, at the gold band that circled my ring finger. I'd worn that ring every day since we'd gotten married, never having once taken it off. I never took it off after Ella passed either. Instead, I wanted to remember all the times we'd shared, even if some hadn't been that great. I rolled the ring around my finger, remembering last night, the words LuAnn and spewed. Instead of leaving it on, I slipped it off.

I gazed down at the tan line where the ring was supposed to be, remembering what LuAnn Billings had said about me out on a date with my dead wife's best friend while still wearing my wedding ring. I walked into the bedroom and opened the small keepsake box on my dresser and dropped the ring inside, then I finished getting dressed.

"What about this one?" Cadence said, stepping up beside one of the pre-cut trees that filled Mindi's lot.

I'd never been so happy when I pulled up outside of the house to see Cadence standing there waiting. She'd smiled and waved and ran over to the truck, climbing in. She'd sat down, turned and handed me a travel mug loaded with hot coffee, then leaned across the truck and placed a kiss on my cheek.

"That's a nice one!" I said, grabbing it and pulling it forward so Cadence could get a better look at it.

"It's really full too, and the perfect shape. It's a little large for my place, but what about yours?" she questioned.

I shrugged. "I guess it would go nicely in the front room."

"Sure would, right in the front window that your mom used to place the tree." Cadence smiled. "Perfect. You get this one. I'm going to get that other one we looked at three trees ago," she said, clapping her hands, going over toward the spot where we'd found the other tree. I yelled over to one of the young kids helping Mindi this year and nodded at him to come over.

Once the trees were loaded into the back of my truck, we made our way out to my place where I'd planned to just drop the tree on the porch. I'd deal with it once I got Cadence back to her place.

"No, you aren't leaving it out here. Please, bring it inside. We can decorate it up," she said, guiding me toward the front door instead of over to the side where I'd planned to put it.

"I don't have any decorations down. Plus, it really should warm up first before we decorate it."

"Nonsense. We take it in, get it in the stand. I'll help you get the decorations. By then it should be warmed a bit."

There was no stopping her. She opened my front door, and we carefully got the tree in my old tree stand. While she filled it with water, I took the stepladder and carefully pulled down a couple of boxes of my old decorations from before I'd been married.

With some Christmas music playing, I placed the lights on the tree, while Cadence poured us some pop and chips and brought them into the living room. Then, while I continued with the lights, she opened one of the boxes of decorations, carefully unwrapping them.

"The tree looks great already," she said, as I flipped the switch, lighting up the tree.

I smiled. "It does." I grabbed one box of decorations and began pulling them out one by one, while she grabbed the other box. Empty boxes strewn on the floor, Cadence carried over the last ornament and placed it on the tree. Then we both stood back looking at the masterpiece we'd decorated.

"It looks great," she said, looking at me to see my reaction.

"It does! Not bad at all!"

"And it finally feels a little Christmassy in here. She walked back over and sat down at the table, noticing a small box sitting in the corner. "Oh gosh, we missed one."

I turned and looked over my shoulder, recognizing the white box instantly. I'd purposely placed that there hoping she wouldn't see it. Panic flooded me, and I was about to tell her not to open it, when she lifted the lid of the box and looked inside. Removing some of the tissue paper, she stopped and lifted her head, her gaze meeting mine.

"Oh, my..." she murmured. Shock lined her face as her cheeks reddened. "I can't believe that you...you kept it?" she stammered.

Embarrassment crept into me while she stared down into the white square box that held an ornament. It was something she shouldn't have seen, and had I been smart, I'd have left it in the storage area. The contents of that box were so precious to me, there would have been no way I could ever have thrown it out. No matter where my life had taken me.

When she looked up at me this time, tears lined her eyes. She carefully reached into the box and pulled out the round glass ornament and ran her fingers over it.

"My cutest little snowflake..." she whispered as she looked down at the ornament. "I remember making this..."

"I remember when you gave it to me, but I could never figure out why that saying was on there. Now, if it had said something like 'the biggest pain in the butt snowflake,' I'd of understood and known it was for me. But saying something nice about the pain-in-the-ass brother's best friend threw me. Did you make another?" I chuckled.

Cadence softly smiled as she looked at the ornament. "No, this was the only one I made."

"Gabe must have pissed you off then. Was that why you didn't give it to your brother?" I replied, knowing that the pair of them were close.

"I can't believe after all these years...you..." she murmured, more to herself than to me, and that was when I realized the truth: that she'd had a crush on me all those years ago also.

"Cadence, was that really made for me?" I asked, my voice low. "Did you..." I stopped. I couldn't ask what I wanted to for fear I was wrong.

The room grew silent while I stood there waiting for her to answer me. My entire body was tense as I waited for a response. Then she looked up at me, her eyes full of tears.

"That was why I had to leave. Why I couldn't hold on to my friendship with Ella. It killed me, knowing..." She put the ornament back into the box and placed it on the table. She looked around in a panic and rushed over to the door where her coat hung on a hook.

I stood there, frozen, realizing what she'd said.

She went to grab her coat but stopped and covered her mouth with her hand. Sobs escaped her covered mouth, and her shoulders shook.

She'd had a crush on me all those years ago. She'd never let go of it either. Just like I hadn't. Instead, I just forced myself to fall in love with someone else because I never thought I could have her. It felt like forever for me to cross the room. I was almost afraid to touch her for fear she'd freak out on me after exposing her feelings toward me. Slowly, I reached out, placing my hands on her shoulders. Her body shook as I pulled her into me. "Why didn't you ever say anything to me?" I questioned, holding her tightly against me.

"Why, to only have my heart broken?" she said, her voice heavy.

"I'd never of broken your heart. Not intentionally anyway."

"Yes, you would have."

"Not a chance. The only reason I never made a move was because of your brother. I wanted you then, and honestly, after seeing you, spending time with you again, I realized that those feelings never left," I said, placing a kiss on the top of her head.

Cadence

December

I pulled out the roast I'd gotten from the grocery store for tonight's dinner from the fridge. I lifted the lid off the roasting pan and set the roast inside, surrounding it with some onion.

Connor had asked that I come over tonight. He'd wanted to prepare the roast for us, but he was needed out in the barn, so I'd come to him instead. I searched the pantry, looking for a couple of spices, when the phone rang.

I grabbed the two jars I'd been looking for and ran out

to grab the phone. "Hello, Darling Ranch," I sang into the phone as I danced around the kitchen to the Christmas song that blasted from the radio on the counter.

"Cadence?" I could barely make out the voice on the other end because of a poor connection. It had been storming most of the day, and it always seemed to affect the phone lines.

"Yes, this is. Who is this?" I questioned, turning down the radio, hoping that I could hear better.

"Gabe."

Excitement ran through me. I'd not heard from my brother since he left. "Gabe!" I screamed in excitement. "Is it really you?" The connection was so bad that I could barely hear him.

"Yeah, Cadence, what are you doing over at Connor's?"

"Making dinner," I replied, as if it were the most normal thing in the world. It was to me anyway. I didn't give him a chance to ask any more questions. "Now tell me, how the hell are you?" I cried, so very excited to hear from my brother.

"I'm good. I wanted to let you know the good news. I'm coming home for Christmas. I tried to call you, but you weren't home." He chuckled. "I didn't expect to find you shacking up with Connor."

He said that to get to me. Instead, I ignored his words

and turned the volume back up on the radio. "Gabe, that is great! I'm very excited to see you."

"Me too, sis, me too. Now, how's everything going?" he questioned. "Do I still have a dairy farm to return home to?"

"Everything is going well. All is good. The house and farm are still standing."

"And Connor?"

I giggled, knowing he'd probably been dying to ask me about that. "Is he's still standing as well? Yes, the last time I checked; he was. He is out in the barn as we speak."

"Okay, listen, pick me up on the 24th at…" Suddenly, the line went dead.

"Gabe? Gabe???" I yelled. Finally, a dial tone beeped in my ear, but Gabe was gone. "Well, shit," I muttered as I hung up the phone.

I walked back over to the counter and continued with the roast just as Connor stepped through the back door. He slipped his feet out of his boots, something he rarely did even at my place when he'd come in for a quick minute and climbed the three steps up the kitchen. Walking over, he wrapped his arms around me and kissed my neck.

"Who were you talking to?" he questioned.

"That was Gabe. He's coming home for Christmas. We got disconnected, so I do not know where to pick him up. All I know is that on the 24th I'm to be somewhere."

"We'll find out. No worries," he said, kissing the column of my neck again.

"That feels so good," I whispered, then picked up one of the spice jars and struggled to open it as he continued kissing me softly.

Since the night we'd decorated the tree, things had gotten a little more physical between us. Our movie nights had turned into make-out sessions, like they would have if we'd been in high school. His hands slid around my waist and rested on the flat of my stomach as his lips moved down to my shoulder.

"Connor." I laughed, still struggling. "I can't open this jar with you...doing this..." I said breathlessly.

"Problem solved," he whispered, his breath tickling my ear as he took the jar from me and placed it down on the counter. Then he pulled me away from there, his hands roaming my body as he continued kissing me.

"Connor, dinner won't get ready if this keeps going," I said, breathless, as he spun me around in his arms and met my lips.

He chuckled then let me go, walked over to the jar and opened it without even a hint of a struggle. "Thank you," I said, taking the jar from his hand and sprinkling the spices on the meat. Once I'd finished and had set the jar back down, Connor went right back to kissing me.

"You almost finished?" he questioned, his hand

drifting under my shirt until his thumb was running over my covered nipple.

I closed my eyes as his touch sent a shiver through me. "Maybe," I said, a little short of breath as his fingers continued dancing over my breast.

"CONNOR....CONNOR..." We heard Joe call.

"Dammit," Connor muttered against my neck, as he quickly adjusted himself. "Keep that thought, would you?" he said, squeezing my side and grinning at me as he shoved his feet back into his boots and grabbed his jacket and hat from the hook on the wall.

"Perhaps I should tell you that."

"Don't worry, I won't forget." He winked, slamming the door shut behind him.

Connor and I sat in his living room, the only light coming from the tree we'd decorated. Soft music played on the radio. I sat on Connor's lap, wineglass in hand, as I told him again about the call I'd received from my brother.

"It will be good to have him back," he said. "We will plan something nice for Christmas Eve. Give him a warm welcome home."

"I'm sure he'd like that," I answered. "Although I

don't think I will let you be in charge of the dessert." I giggled, looking over at the mess that was supposed to be a chocolate cheesecake.

"Hey, I never claimed to be a great baker," Connor said, holding up his hands. "I was supposed to look after the roast, remember? You were supposed to make the dessert," he said, his hand gripping my side, tickling me.

I pushed at his hands, almost spilling my wine. He quickly took the wineglass from me and set it on the table. "So, tell me again, why you didn't make the dessert?" He gripped my side, causing me to burst out into a fit of laughter once again.

Again, I tried pushing his hand off me, only this time he gripped my free hand with his, rendering me useless. I squirmed and laughed as he tickled me until I almost couldn't breathe.

"Okay, okay...I'm sorry." I laughed breathlessly. "Next time...I'll stick to dessert."

"You better. I mean, I love dessert but clearly can't make it." He laughed as he continued to tickle me.

The tickling slowed as Connor looked down at me. Somehow, we'd shifted around until I was lying on the couch, almost underneath him. He was beside me, and his blue eyes stared down into mine. He slowly released my hand, slowly bringing his other one up to my cheek. The smile fell from his face and a look I'd never seen on him before coming into view.

He slowly brought his lips to mine, kissing me hard. His hand rested now on my hip where only moments ago he'd been tickling me. Now I felt the rough skin of his fingers stroke my bare skin just above the waistband of my pants as he assaulted my mouth.

With each swipe of his tongue against mine, I felt him grow harder. I closed my eyes and allowed myself to get lost in his kiss, my hands now running up under his shirt. I bit my bottom lip and tilted my head back as his lips moved down the front of my neck.

"Connor," I breathed, feelings running through my body that were foreign to me, as I felt his hardness through his pants.

He pushed my shirt up and over my head, tossing it to the floor. His eyes met mine, and I watched as his gaze skimmed my body. He bent down and kissed my collarbone. Slowly, he trailed kisses all the way down between my breasts while his large hands held them, his thumbs brushing over my hardened nipples.

His touch felt different tonight. His look was different. For the first time since we'd started messing around, tonight felt different. I closed my eyes and ran my hands through his thick hair as I succumbed to his touch.

"Not hear," he muttered and stood up from the couch, holding his hand out for me to take.

"What?" I muttered as he pulled me up.

"Come with me," he whispered, bending down and

grabbing my shirt off the floor then leading me upstairs. Shoving open the bedroom door, he pulled me into him, kissing me. He kicked the door shut behind him and gently guided me over to the bed. "Our first time isn't going to be on a couch."

I closed my eyes and allowed myself to get lost in his touch. His rough fingers traced up my arms and around to my back, where he pinched the clasp of my bra together, removing it in one quick motion. I felt the fabric fall away from my body, the chill in the air instantly causing my nipples to harden.

"God, you're beautiful," he whispered, taking my mouth with his as he wrapped his arms around me and pulled me in close.

I ran my hands up his strong, muscular back as his tongue washed through my mouth again. He stepped back, reached behind him, and pulled his shirt off over his head. Then he quickly flicked the button of his jeans open. The look in his eyes was one of want and need as he approached me. His hands went right for my jeans, prying them open. As he removed my jeans, his fingers trailed down my body, his touch sending waves of excitement through me.

My gaze fell to his hard cock, large and thick as he pushed his jeans off to the side. He approached the bed, my heart beating so hard I could feel it in my throat. Licking my lips, my gaze met his as I took him in my hand, gently stroking his cock before bringing him to my lips. The second he was in my mouth, I felt his fingers grip my hair. I took him as far back as I could, where I could feel the head of his cock throb against the back of my throat.

The low, guttural groan that escaped his lips as I ran my tongue around him caused me to clench my legs together. I'd hoped that by doing so it would ease the want I was feeling there, but it did little good. I took him to the back of my throat again as he gripped my hair tighter.

I closed my eyes, relishing the feel of his large hand on the back of my head, the taste of him as I moved him in and out of my mouth.

"Fuck," he hissed. "Feels so amazing," he breathed, his abs clenching tight.

I pulled him from my mouth for a moment, trying to relax my jaw from his size, but as soon as I did, he grabbed hold of me and shoved me down on the bed. He knelt onto the floor, gripped the band of my panties, and pulled them down, then rested my legs on either side of his head. He kissed his way up the inside of my thighs, a soft moan escaping from my mouth, before he connected his mouth to my center.

His fingers interlocked with mine as his tongue found that sensitive little bud that he alternated lapping and sucking. I lifted my head, watching him. It was almost my undoing when he lifted his eyes to meet mine. My head fell back to the mattress as he continued lapping and sucking at my center until my legs began shaking.

I felt the mattress move, his weight shifting me, as he made his way onto the bed. He hovered over me, meeting my eyes. He brought his lips to mine. His kiss was now slower and less demanding than before. He reached over to the nightstand, pulling the drawer open, and fished around inside, pulling out a condom.

He ripped the package open and slipped it on, grabbing both my legs and resting them on his hips. Lining himself up with me, he once again met my lips as he pushed himself inside me. I shifted uncomfortably for a moment, trying hard to steady my breath at his intrusion.

"You okay?" he asked breathlessly.

"Mmm, yes."

He pushed himself inside of me, stopping every few seconds to allow me to relax around him until he was finally deep inside of me. His kiss was now tender as he moved inside of me at a slow pace.

"How does that feel?" His breath tickled my ear.

I moaned, closing my eyes, allowing myself to feel him —every inch of him—buried inside of me. "So good," I moaned.

He held himself up on one arm as his other hand gripped my ass, moving me a little to position us differently. Moving me enough that it felt like he went deeper inside of me.

"I've...I've wanted this for so...long," he said, his breathing ragged.

I closed my eyes as he brought his lips to mine. I could feel my orgasm building as I gripped his arm. His muscles flexed under my hand, his breathing growing more ragged as he, too, was nearing his release.

Connor

I opened my eyes, my bedroom coming into focus. I lay there, my body completely relaxed, and let out a yawn. Cadence lay in my arms, her back pressed against my chest. I pressed a kiss to her bare shoulder as I pulled her closer to me. I closed my eyes, the memory of last night came to my mind, how our bodies fit so perfectly together, how she felt as her body released her orgasm.

I never thought that I'd feel anything this intense again. Cadence shifted in my arms, rolling over and snuggling into my chest.

"Morning," she whispered, pressing her lips against my peck.

"Morning." I tilted her head back so I could place a kiss on her lips.

She softly smiled as she looked into my eyes. Her eyes

said everything. She was just as in love with me as I was with her, I could see it. I wanted to tell her how I felt, but I didn't want her to run from me. She rested her hand on my chest and then ran it down to my already hardened cock.

I sucked in a breath as she stroked me. I gripped her hand, stopping her, and rolled over, resting my weight on my forearm, and looked down into her face.

"What are you trying to do? Are you trying to get me going again?" I asked, pressing my lips to hers as we both laughed.

"Maybe," she answered, looking up at me with a hint of playfulness in her eyes.

"Are you sure you should start this?" I asked, running my hand down the side of her body, positioning her leg on my hip. I'd realized quickly last night that she really liked this position. She'd especially liked it when rolled her over and pulled her on top of me.

She nodded her head and kissed me hard, moving my hand to her breast.

"You are bad," I whispered as I began kissing my way down her body.

I was just about to her stomach when I heard what sounded like the back door slam downstairs. Looking up, I listened, but Cadence had other ideas. She gripped my chin, pulling my attention back to her.

"It's probably just Joe coming in for something," she said, her voice low. "Just ignore it. Put your focus here."

I allowed my eyes to drift to where she held her breasts in her hands. God, she was the most beautiful thing as she lay there watching me with that look of want and need in her eyes. I lowered my head to her belly and continued kissing her. I shifted myself lower in the bed and allowed her to rest her legs on my shoulders. I took my time, kissing and biting the inside of her thighs, and I was just about to connect with her center when what sounded like a dish broke downstairs. My head shot up, pulling my attention from her.

"What the fuck?" I bit out, jumping from the bed.

Cadence sat up, pulling the covers up around her. "What was that?" she asked, panic lining her voice.

"You heard that, right?" I asked, keeping my voice low.

She nodded her head, looking around for her shirt, which was over by the door. "Who'd be here?"

"Stay here." I grabbed my shirt from the floor and threw it over my head and then reached for my flannel pajama pants that were hanging off the end of the bed. "I'll be right back."

"Connor, be careful," I heard her whisper.

"Don't worry, I will be," I said as I cautiously walked out of the bedroom, peeking down the stairs. I'd hoped to see whoever it was before they heard or saw me, but I couldn't. I looked over my shoulder at Cadence, who sat wrapped in the blankets, looking petrified. God, I hated to leave her, but I pulled the door shut and quietly made my way down the stairs.

I got to the foot of the stairs when I heard voices mumbling in the kitchen, sounding almost like arguing. I made a point of making enough noise to alert whoever it was before I stepped into the kitchen.

"There you are!" Paula said, throwing her arms in the air. "I told you he was here."

Bill turned and nodded at me. "Hope we didn't wake you. It's not like you to still be in bed this late in the day," he said, glancing at his watch.

I looked up at the clock and frowned. "What are you guys doing here? I thought you weren't coming until mid-month?"

"Connor, dear, don't be silly. It's the fourteenth. It is mid-month."

I glanced at my wall calendar; it was indeed the fourteenth. I'd even circled the date with black marker, so I didn't forget. I turned and looked back at Bill and Paula and nodded. "Guess it is." I shrugged.

"Are you sick, Connor?" Paula asked, stepping forward and placing her hand on my forehead. "Ella always said you were up before the sunrise. Her being gone has really affected the way you function, hasn't it? That's okay, it has for me too. Don't worry, we will get you back to waking before the roosters," she said, moving toward the coffeemaker to brew a pot of coffee.

I heard the floor creak above my head and sat down at the kitchen table, my cheeks heating as guilt flooded through me. What would Bill and Paula say when Cadence appeared?

"Connor, you look a little flush. You sure you're feeling okay?" Paula questioned as she looked over at me. "Bill, I think he may be sick."

Bill stopped unloading my dishwasher and looked over at me. "He looks a little flushed. Perhaps he should visit the town doctor. I can take him in an hour," Bill added, reaching for more dishes.

"I don't need a doctor," I bit out. I really wanted to go back upstairs to be with Cadence and forget that they were here. In reality, all I needed to do was get up there and warn her before she came down.

Just then, Paula glanced toward the back door as it slammed shut. I frowned, looking over in the same direction to see a blond-haired woman step into my kitchen. I'd never seen her before but could tell instantly that she knew both Bill and Paula. She stepped up into the kitchen and walked over beside Paula, finally looking at me.

"What the hell is going on?" I roared.

"Connor, meet Olivia. We were really hoping that this year would be special," she said, stepping over toward this woman who stood in my kitchen.

I glanced over at her. She couldn't have been any more than twenty-two or twenty-three. A kid really. I frowned. "You wanted what to be special?" I glanced over at Bill, who stood there looking proud.

"Connor, meet my sister's daughter. She lived with her father out in the Midwest and has finally come home to her mother's place. You may know her mother, LuAnn Billings. Anyway, Olivia has had a recent string of bad luck in the love department, so I offered to introduce the pair of you."

"Introduce us?" I roared, my anger getting the best of me. "What are you talking about?"

"See Bill, this is why I didn't mention anything. I knew he would instantly tell me not to bother bringing her."

"You're damn right I would have."

"That is why I decided to surprise you. Bill said you'd probably be angry at that, but I figured it was better to ask for forgiveness than ask for permission."

This was all just too much for me to handle at the moment. I wanted to rewind time, to go back up to bed. I wiped my face with my hand and sighed. When I looked back over at Paula, who stood beside Olivia, I noticed she was staring at something behind me, a funny look on her face. "Paula, are you..."

When she didn't acknowledge me, I turned around to see Cadence standing in the kitchen doorway wearing one of my T-shirts, nothing more. Her eyes were glassy as she stared at Paula, then Olivia, and then at me.

"Get dressed," I muttered, not an ounce of warmth in my voice. The situation before me had pissed me off too much to be anything but cold. The instant the words had flown from my mouth and I saw the look in her eyes, I knew it was the wrong way to handle the situation. Especially after the night we'd spent together, but I didn't have a choice. Bill and Paula had always made me feel on edge. Now was no different. Especially now as I turned back to face both Bill, Paula, and now Olivia.

"Connor, what is Cadence doing here...dressed... dressed...like...." Paula covered her mouth as her eyes filled with tears.

"Like some whore," Olivia interrupted.

Anger flowed through me. Who did she think she was coming into my home and treating anyone that way? "That is enough out of you," I yelled, staring her in the eyes, letting her know I meant what I'd said. "Bill and Paula, I'm sorry. I should have mentioned something to you."

"Are you sleeping with her?" Paula asked, anger spreading over her face.

As Bill and Paula stood there looking at me, I knew I'd gone about this all wrong. What did I think they would say when they found out Cadence and I were together? Hell, she and Ella had been best friends. I'd seen the way

Paula had hugged her when she'd returned to Willow Valley for the funeral. It was the same way she would have hugged her own daughter. They'd treated Cadence like one of their own. Even I knew that. Then my thoughts switched immediately to Cadence. What was she going to think as I stood here facing Ella's parents?

"Look, I'm sorry—"

"You should be sorry. Honestly, I'm going to pretend that I didn't just see Cadence in your T-shirt in the doorway because—"

Paula stopped speaking as we all heard the front door slam. I didn't bother caring what they thought as I ran through the house to the front door. I shoved my feet into my shoes and took off toward Cadence as she made her way to the truck.

Grabbing her, I spun her around. "Wait a minute," I said, finally meeting her eyes, trying to catch my breath.

"Connor, please...I need to go," she cried, her voice shaking as she looked at me.

"No. I won't let you. They shouldn't even be here, not this way..." I said, trying to hold on to her.

"And Olivia..." she muttered, her bottom lip now shaking as tears streamed down her face.

"You know her?" I questioned, shocked, because in all the years I'd been with Ella, I'd never laid eyes on her.

"Oh, I know her all right. Remember how I told you about Daniel? That is the Olivia," she cried.

I was in such shock, I barely even processed what she said. What kind of messed-up world was this? Bill and Paula had brought her to me to fix us up? I didn't want anyone but Cadence.

Panic hit me as I realized that it was the same girl who'd messed with Cadence's relationship before. I knew she'd probably heard every word Paula said regarding fixing us up, so to her it probably felt like another personal attack. First Ella, and now, once again, her cousin. She was probably worried I'd turn my sights on her, just like Daniel had done.

"Apparently, she is a sought-after piece. I hope you are very happy together," Cadence bit out.

Before I could stop her, Cadence was in her truck. I was about to approach her, rip open the door, and take her inside the house where I could stand up for the pair of us. Instead, she spun the wheels and took off.

I'd wanted to go after her, but first I needed to deal with the mess that was now inside my home. I took a few minutes to come to my senses before I walked back in through the front door. When I did, I was about to kick my shoes off when I looked up to see Paula and Bill step into the living room.

"Connor, perhaps we should have called first," Bill said, guiding his wife over to the couch. "Made sure that it was okay that we introduce you to Olivia...that you were ready to move on..."

I rolled my eyes, then I too moved into the room. I took a seat across from them, trying to form my thoughts before I spoke.

Paula leaned over to Bill. "Clearly, we should have called first. I'd of thought that a year would be enough, but perhaps I was wrong..."

"What world are you people living in?" I yelled.

Bill and Paula looked over at me, confusion on their faces. "What?"

"Look. Ever since Ella died, you have taken every opportunity you could to remind me of the fact that she died alone, that perhaps I could have saved her, that perhaps I could have done more. LuAnn even took out an article in the paper trying to pin her death on me. Don't think I don't know it, because I do. I read the damn thing. It had her written all over it."

"What?" Paula asked, shocked. "Why would she do that?"

"For the same reason she was harassing Cadence and I the other night. She's not right."

"LuAnn wouldn't do anything of the kind," Paula said, going to stand up and come over to me.

"No, don't play these games. You know what I am saying is the truth. With LuAnn and yourself. Every single chance you've had, you've reminded me of all these things. I realized I was staying in the zone I was in because everyone else didn't want me to move on."

"Yes...and we've brought a lovely young woman for you to meet."

"Paula, Bill, all due respect, but I don't want to meet someone you are fixing me up with. Olivia doesn't fall far from the tree of her mother. Ask her what she did to Cadence a few years ago."

"Don't be ridiculous. Cadence and Olivia have never met. Ella only met her one time, when they were about four. That was when Olivia went to live with her father."

"Well, they have met. Olivia was friends with Cadence when she was living with her grandparents. It seemed Olivia had a fondness for Cadence's boyfriend."

"No way. Not our Olivia," Paula said.

"Yes Paula, your Olivia. I know you don't believe me, so why don't you just see what she has to say?"

"I'm not going to ask her something like that because I know she'd never do anything like that. Her mother raised her better than that."

"Whatever you say." I muttered under my breath. "Well, it doesn't matter because I want you to note, and you'd better take it seriously, I've met the woman I want to be with."

"Connor, you can't be serious," Paula said. "Cadence is...well...she's Cadence."

I nodded. "Yes, she is Cadence, and I love everything about her." I took a moment, thinking about the words I'd just spoken. "Perhaps you should have called before you came out here at the crack of dawn. That way you could have found out about us the proper way, and not with her showing up in nothing but my T-shirt."

"Connor, please, just think about this," Bill said, sitting forward.

"Think about what? That I should only move when you tell me to? I'm sorry, you may have had that kind of hold over your daughter, but you don't have it over me. You may like to think you do, and for a while I may have allowed it, but it won't happen again. That was my mistake," I said, feeling the weight I'd been carrying for months lift from my chest.

The room grew quiet as the three of us sat there, staring at one another. The tension in the room was palpable. I was worried about how Bill and Paula would take this; I was worried about how Cadence was dealing with everything, and I wanted nothing more than to be there to help her realize everything was fine.

"Connor, we never meant to harm you intentionally," Paula said, tears filling her eyes.

"Intentional or not, the hurt was done. We both lost someone, we both have grieved, but now I need to pick up the pieces and move on. I won't live my life alone."

I got up out of the chair and went to leave the room. I needed to get over and see Cadence, to make sure she was okay. I was just about to climb the stairs when I heard Paula say my name. I turned around to see her wiping her eyes.

"What?"

"We will be out of your way. Just give us some time to calm down."

As I looked over at Paula, who buried her head into her husband's shoulder, I felt bad. Just like her words had hurt me, mine had hurt them. It hadn't been my intention; I was angry. I didn't need anyone to tell me who I should or shouldn't love. "Paula, you guys don't have to leave. I'd never, ever turn either of you away."

"Really? Even though we really haven't been that fair to you. I never realized that you took what I'd said to heart."

I looked around the room. They'd been more than fair to me in some ways. They'd help me repair this place when otherwise I'd have lost it.

"Paula, how could I not? I blamed myself for months over her death. Months. Then to realize that you both thought it too broke my heart. I loved Ella very much, and it's taken me a long time to heal. It's taken me a long time to be okay with knowing I needed to move on. I can't even begin to repay you for the money you gave me. You sold your family cottage, for goodness' sake," I said, tears coming to my eyes, remembering how I felt when they'd told me they had taken care of all my home and farm repairs. "Please know, I'd never turn my back on either of you. You are more than welcome in my home; you are my family. But that means that you also treat my new girl-friend, or wife when and if the time comes, with the same respect you'd show when your own daughter was alive.

Paula looked over at me and got up. Coming over, she wrapped her arms around me and cried. "Connor, we are so sorry. I wish you had said something to me earlier."

I wrapped my arms around Paula and placed a kiss on her cheek. "Me too. This clearly wasn't the way to do it." I chuckled as I hugged her a little tighter. "Now, if you'll excuse me, I am going to make sure that Cadence is okay."

"Of course."

I'd come home, started a fire, and now sat in the quiet of my living room. I'd finally stopped crying after making myself some coffee. What had I been thinking, sleeping with Connor? I should have known better, I thought as I sat down with my mug and a plate of fruit. I heard him apologizing to Bill and Paula as if I'd been nothing but a huge mistake. I should have known he wasn't ready. He'd never be ready because, no matter what, the feelings I had for him were greater and far older than the ones he had for me. He may be older, just like he was in school, but the feelings he held for me would never catch up to mine. I knew that now.

I'd debated what to do on the way home. I'd decided that I'd go back out to my grandparents' place once Gabe arrived home. There was no need for me to stay here any longer. I'd decided that once I finished my coffee, I'd pack my stuff, then I'd call the real estate agent who carried the listing and cancel it. I'd move back there and be done with the entire situation. I was done with Willow Valley.

My throat hurt from all the crying I'd done on the way home. I swallowed a mouthful of hot coffee and sat down beside the fire when the phone rang. I didn't recognize the number, so I answered.

"Cadence, this is Jonathan Hall, from Hall Realty. I'd like to let you know that there has been an offer on the farm. I know it's taken a while, but you will be happy to know it came in over asking."

I said nothing; I felt totally numb at this news, just as I had when I stepped inside the front door. This was the last thing I wanted to hear because I knew I'd really have nowhere to go now.

"Just say the word and I will send you over the offer, but considering the offer itself, I'd be surprised if you denied it. Looks good to me, so, look at it and ask questions, should you have any."

I didn't want to look at an offer. Hell, I wasn't even sure what I was doing. What I wanted was to ask him if it was too late to pull out, but I knew it was. Instead, without thinking, I shoved a piece of apple into my mouth. "You know what, if it's that good, just accept it. Send over whatever it is you need signed," I muttered, then hung up.

I took a sip of my drink when the phone rang once more. Figuring it was Jonathon again, I answered, to hear my brother's voice on the other end.

"Cadence how are you?" he questioned.

"Fine," I replied.

"I'm flying in on the 23rd now. Can you pick me up at the town hall?"

I swallowed hard, tears forming in my eyes. I needed to get out of Willow Valley, and I needed to do it soon. I could feel it. I couldn't stay here. My heart hurt, my chest hurt, my heart had been broken and the longer I kept things inside, the worse it was going to get.

"Cadence, is everything okay?" Gabe asked.

I'd just realized I hadn't said a word to him about his change of flight.

That was it. The sound of his voice made me crack and tears streamed down my face. "No. I'm not okay. Everything is not fine."

"What is it?" he asked. "What's wrong?" I could hear the concern in his voice.

"I need to go. I have to leave Willow Valley. I told you it was a mistake coming here."

Gabe cleared his throat and whispered something to someone before returning to the phone. "Cadence, tell me what is going on?"

I looked around the room, at the Christmas tree that stood in the corner, reminding me of the night Conner and I had decorated it. Then I glanced over to the couch, to where we'd gotten halfway through a movie before we'd started making out. Then I thought to this morning, to the cold look in his eyes as he barked at me to get dressed. I sniffled, reaching for a tissue from the box on the table in front of me.

"I'm...I'm heartbroken Gabe. Connor and I, well, let's just say the plan you orchestrated worked."

"Wonderful, that makes me so happy...but..." He stopped as the weight of my words sunk in. "If it worked, why are you heartbroken?" Gabe asked.

I pulled another tissue from the box and blew my nose. "His feelings for me will never catch up to mine. That's why. Ella's parents...that's another reason." I blew my nose again.

"Cadence, you aren't making an ounce of sense to me."

I got up and began pacing the room. Then I ran up to my bedroom and pulled my suitcase out from under the bed and began throwing my clothes inside.

"Keep up, would you? I just got a call from the real estate guy. The farm has sold. I was hoping to take it off the market, but I got the call before I could. I was going to go back there. Now I have no clue where I'll go."

I heard Gabe let out a deep breath. I imagined he was running his hand through his messy hair, wondering to himself why his sister had to be such a basket case over every little thing. Why I couldn't cope with things the way he could.

"Cadence, why are you going anywhere?"

"I guess I'll just move to Florida. Most everyone whose life is over moves to Florida. Yeah, Florida would be fine," I muttered more to myself.

"Cadence, please calm down. Don't be irrational. Just wait it out a few days, wait for me to come home, then we can talk this through. I'm sure it's not as bad as it seems."

I laughed under my breath. Did he really just call me irrational? Me? "I'm not irrational, Gabe," I said through clenched teeth.

"You aren't?"

"No! What did I do when I heard Connor was getting married? I didn't act irrational."

Gabe laughed. "Sorry, sis, but moving out and to the Midwest isn't something one does on a whim."

"I didn't do it on a whim. Grams and Gramps needed me and you know it."

"Perhaps they did, maybe they didn't. Perhaps you were looking for an out. Regardless, getting up and moving without so much as a second thought is irrational to me," Gabe replied.

Irritation grew inside of me. "I have to go. I don't have time to listen to this."

"Cadence, wait," I heard as I went to place the phone down.

"What?"

"Where are you going to go? Back to the Midwest?"

I stood there, looking around the mess in my room. I'd pulled clothes from the closet and from drawers with no type of order in mind, and they were now a heap of a mess in my suitcase.

"I don't know. The Midwest isn't far enough. Florida sounds nice, but...maybe Canada, Alaska...France?"

"God, Cadence, irrationality at its finest. Seriously, do nothing until I get home. I've got to go."

"Call Connor. Tell him to pick you up. I'll see you when I see you," I said, hanging up and focusing on the task in front of me: packing and getting out of Willow Valley as quickly as I could.

After the confrontation with Bill and Paula, they fought while I took a shower and got dressed. I rushed down the stairs and out the front door. My world was literally crashing down around me with each second I waited to go to Cadence. I was almost to my truck when I heard the front door slam behind me.

"Connor, can I speak with you a moment before you go?" Bill yelled.

"What?" I yelled back, irritated that I'd not gotten away faster. "What is it you need?" I asked, turning around to face him.

"I'd like to have a word with you for a moment if I could," Bill said, stepping down off the porch.

I let out a breath and looked my father-in-law in the eyes. "What?" I didn't mean to be short, but I knew time was slipping away. I knew Cadence and her irrational thought pattern. She'd already been gone long enough to pack her stuff and already be heading for the Midwest.

"I'm sure you probably heard Paula and I yelling earlier. We have been having this disagreement for months."

"I see." I said, crossing my arms.

"It was her idea to bring Olivia. Not mine. I want you to know that. I told her it would be better if she asked first, but she insisted. She kept telling me there was no way you were seeing anyone."

"Okay." I really wasn't sure what it was he was trying to say, but I could tell from the seriousness of his tone and the look in his eyes that it was important for him to say it.

"Paula felt, and has felt, for a long time that you were just going to go out as quickly as you could and replace Ella. I told her she was being ridiculous."

I couldn't believe my ears. Why would she think that? When had I ever alluded to me not loving my wife in the years I was with her? I just stood there, kept quiet and listened. I was tired of arguing, and I still had one battle to fight. It was one I knew would take up a lot of my energy and focus.

"I always stood up for you. I'd ask her why she felt that way, but she could never answer me. The last couple of times on the phone with you, she was so horrible, so I finally started throwing her own words back at her. She'd always say she loved you like a son, but yet here she was saying all these horrible things."

"I appreciate you standing up for me."

Bill nodded. "I want you to be happy. We want you to be happy. I mean, hell, I've lived my life. It's only fair you live yours."

"Yet Paula doesn't agree?"

"Now she does. It's not a secret that she has been having a really hard time with all this. She was looking for anyone to blame, anyone at all that may give her a reason she lost her daughter. Is it right? No, but that is what she has done."

"I appreciate you being honest with me."

Bill nodded, then looked me in the eye. "We want nothing more than for you to be happy. So, for what it is worth, we want you to know that you have our blessing. We both love Cadence like a daughter, and I think it shocked Paula and I both to see you with her."

I nodded. "Thank you. Now, I've got to go."

I was almost to the end of my driveway when my cell phone rang. Praying it was Cadence, I came to a stop and answered.

"Hello, Cadence, please tell me it's you."

"Connor? Connor, it's Gabe. Where are you?"

"Gabe?" I asked, placing my phone down on the seat beside me, turning my truck out onto the road. I couldn't waste any more time. I'd messed things up enough, now I needed to make it right.

"Yeah, I just, I wanted to call you. See what the hell is going on back there. I spoke with Cadence. She's really upset, man. I'm scared she is going to do something irrational."

I frowned, feeling the weight of what had happened on my shoulders. I knew I'd gone about everything wrong. I should have thrown them out. I should have treated Cadence a lot differently than I did when she'd appeared in the doorway of my kitchen. I should have protected her from them. At least from the daggers they threw at her, but I'd barked. I'd been a complete ass to the woman I'd wanted for years, instead of showing her the respect she deserved.

"Yeah, I was afraid of that."

"Afraid of what? Would someone please tell me what the fuck is going on back there?" he barked. "I've listened to Cadence speak in code, without really telling me what is going on. Don't you start on me also."

"God, Gabe. Don't hate me. I..."

I kept my focus on the road ahead. I knew I needed to

man up and tell my best friend what happened, and I had to do it now.

"I slept with Cadence."

I could already see him blowing up. It was a good thing he was miles away from Willow Valley, or I'd end up just like Paul Longshire. I'd be beaten and bloodied, crying on the pavement as Gabe gave me exactly what I'd deserved.

"Thank god! It's about time," Gabe said into the phone.

"Fuck, I know, I'm sorry...it just sort of... What did you just say?" I questioned.

"I said, it's about time!" Gabe chuckled into the phone.

I could barely believe what I was hearing. Was he really happy that we'd.... that we'd...slept together?

"Now, tell me, why is she all upset?"

"I blew it, man... I fucked up. I didn't protect her the way I should have this morning when Bill and Paula showed up."

The look I'd given her when I'd seen her in my T-shirt, peeking into the kitchen, was eating at me. My cold bark telling her to get dressed made me feel like an asshole—the asshole I was being because of the situation that had presented itself.

"Tell me what happened," Gabe said, pulling me back from my thoughts.

"Bill and Paula showed up. I knew they were coming. I lost track of the days. They arrived while Cadence and I were still in bed..."

"Enough said," Gabe replied. "I know how they've treated you during the whole entire time regarding Ella, so I'm sure I can already see where this is going."

Gabe had known everything that had happened when it had come to Bill and Paula. He was the only one I felt I could talk to, because he'd been witness to it. I grew quiet as I drove down the road. I knew my best friend didn't want to hear about me doing his sister, and I'd have to apologize later but right now, I needed his help.

"I can't lose her, man," I said as I turned into their driveway. "I just can't."

"You won't."

"I dunno. She was heartbroken, Gabe. I tried to talk to her before she left the house, but she refused. I've never seen her look so hurt because of something I'd done. If you'd have seen her face..."

"Talk to her. Or try. Are you on the way over now?" Gabe questioned, worry thick in his voice.

"I am. Just turned into the driveway now."

"If she isn't there, can you please promise me, no matter what happens, that you'll pick me up on the 23rd at town hall?" Gabe questioned. "Hopefully, between the pair of us, we will find out where she is, if she isn't at home. Then we can go get her together."

"Yeah, I will be there. Got to go," I said, hanging up.

I pulled up out front of the house. The first thing I noticed was the missing truck. She had to still be here. There was no way she could have left this fast. What was I saying, this was Cadence. This girl had packed and moved in less than twelve hours when her grandparents called. I cut the engine and ran up to the front door. I turned the handle to find the door was locked, so I banged hard, shouting for Cadence.

I waited and waited, but she didn't answer. I looked around. Perhaps she parked behind the house. I took off, running to the back of the house. Had she hidden her truck back there, so I'd think she was gone? Was she playing me? But as I rounded the corner of the house, I noticed that her truck wasn't there either. Defeat filled me, as well as worry. I was about to make my way back to the front porch when one of the farmhands I'd not worked with yet approached me.

"Can I help you?" he asked.

"Have you seen Cadence?"

"Yep, she left about half an hour ago. Said something to me about making sure we take care of things before we left for the day. Didn't really say anything else. Seemed a little distraught."

"Did she say where she was headed?" I asked, looking out toward the front of the house in case she was coming back down the driveway.

"Depends on who is asking?"

I frowned, looking at this young kid. Annoyed, I looked down into his face. "Where is Jack?" I barked. I wasn't in the mood for games. Plus, he was annoying me.

"I said, who's asking?" this kid asked, puffing out his chest.

I clenched my fists at my side and was about to take a tone when I heard a familiar voice. "Hey, Connor. Everything okay?" Jack asked, coming over to us.

"Have you seen Cadence?"

Jack looked at the other farmhand and nodded toward the barn. "Get back to work."

The kid took off in the direction of the barn as he was told, and Jack looked at me. "She was here. She left in a hurry, seemed upset and a little distraught. I tried to talk to her, but she said she had to go. Told me I was to take care of things until Gabe came home. It was weird, Connor. I was going to call you, but I got busy with things in the barn."

"Don't worry about it. Did you notice if she took anything with her, a bag?"

Jack shook his head. "Not that I know of. Is she all right?"

"Not sure," I said, heading toward my truck. Anger coursed through me. "Call me if she returns at any point!" I yelled back to him and climbed into my truck.

Cadence

My eyes were red and swollen from all the tears I'd cried. I sat in my truck outside of Bluebird Books, trying to calm myself before going inside. I took a sip of the latte I'd just picked up and relaxed my head against my seat. My head was pounding, and my eyes hurt. I needed to figure out what my next steps were going to be. I could always drive out to the airport, grab a flight somewhere, and just figure it out once I land, I thought to myself. Or I could just go back to my grandparents', take my time cleaning up the rest of the items in the house, and go from there.

I glanced in the rearview mirror, my bag still sat in the back seat of the truck. I'd packed it and shoved it in there while a mix of hurt and anger coursed through me. Perhaps they had reopened the inn, I thought to myself.

Maybe just hiding away there for a few days would do me good. Give me time to figure things out.

I glanced at my watch. Whatever I was going to do, I needed to decide. I grabbed my cup and my purse and climbed out of the truck. First thing I knew I needed to do was to grab a book on a couple places I figured I could go.

I stepped into the small bookstore and noticed that both Trinity and Peggy were sitting enjoying tea together. There was one other person shopping inside. I nodded to both of them and walked over to the travel section.

"Cadence, right?" Peggy questioned.

"Yes." I did my best to give her a smile.

"Anything I can help you find?" Trinity asked, getting up from the chair she was seated in.

I looked up at the wall of books and ran my fingers over the spines. "I'm looking for a couple books, one on Florida and the other on..." I quickly skimmed the names of states and countries on the spines of the books and then blurted, "Canada."

Trinity gave me a funny look and nodded. "Okay, Florida and... Canada."

I watched as she ran her fingers over the books, pulling out two or three different ones on each place. "Here we are. Florida and Canada," she said, handing me two separate piles.

"Thank you," I muttered.

"Take a seat, peruse those books. Make sure they are

what you are looking for before you buy them, dear," she said, pointing to a large wingback chair against the window. "I want to make sure they contain the information you are looking for." She smiled.

I walked over, noticing a small black cat curled up on the back of the chair. I almost didn't want to sit down for fear of disturbing her.

"Don't worry about Luna," Peggy said. "She loves people and loves that chair. You may be her new best friend." She winked.

"Thanks," I said as I sat down on the edge of the chair and placed the books in my lap. I'd flipped through the first book and placed it beside me, starting in the next one.

"So, do you mind if I ask what made you choose those locations? I mean, they are in the exact opposite direction of one another." Peggy said.

I looked over and saw both ladies were looking at me, curiosity in their eyes.

"Well, I um...I need a change of scenery. A new start... if you will," I said, continuing to flip through the books.

"Oh, I thought you were going to settle here?" Trinity said, taking a sip of her drink.

"Me too," I muttered, my mind going back to Connor. It was then my eyes got blurry. I wiped at them, quickly removing the tears that were building in them.

"My dear, is everything all right?" Trinity asked,

coming over to me with a box of tissues. "Here, take one, please."

I quickly took two and thanked her, blowing my nose and wiping my eyes before I looked over at them. "How did you know something was wrong?"

"Oh goodness, dear, you look like you've just lost everything you ever had. We are happy to listen if you need to talk. We don't pry. Whatever we talk about stays between these four walls."

"Thank you," I whispered, closing the book in my lap. They both went back to talking between themselves while I sat there looking down at my choices. Neither of them was right. I knew that. I'd had a sick feeling inside of me ever since I asked for the two locations. I didn't really want to go anywhere; I wanted to stay right where I was, in the arms of the man I loved.

I stood up and went over to them. "Do you have a moment?" I questioned.

Both the women looked at me and nodded.

"I think I need a new start. Yet, as I sit here looking through those books, my heart is screaming at me."

Peggy and Trinity looked at one another and nodded. "What do you think that means?" Peggy asked.

I shrugged. I had no clue what it meant. I knew that I wasn't ready to face it though. I wasn't ready to learn what that meant. "I have not got a clue, but I'm not sure I'm really ready to hear it either."

"My dear, at least you know you don't want to admit it to yourself."

I sighed. They were right, I didn't. "Do you know if the inn is back open yet?" I questioned. Perhaps if I could just stay the night in a neutral environment, not one that was going to cloud my sight, it would be better.

"No, it's not. I heard it was going up for sale, unfortunately. Why do you ask?"

I softly smiled. "Well, I figured maybe I'd stay there for the night. You know, to clear my head."

Trinity looked over at Peggy, and both ladies turned to me. They'd seen me around town with Connor, at both the fall fair and the tree lighting. I wasn't stupid; I knew they knew it had to do with us.

"Cadence, does this have something to do with Connor?"

That was it. His name was all I needed to hear. I'd held myself together for so long, and then they'd said his name. I buried my face into my hands and wept in the middle of the store, in front of two women I barely knew.

"Oh dear. Come sit down." I felt one of them put their arms around me and guide me over to a chair. "Now, talk to us."

A tissue box was again thrust at me, and I took a couple more, again blowing my nose and wiping my eyes.

"Gosh, I feel so silly," I cried.

"Nonsense. We've all been through it. If these walls

could talk, they'd tell you exactly that. So, tell us your story."

I sat there in that small bookstore spilling my guts to two women I didn't know. They each sat there listening as I shared with them the events that had led up to this moment. When I'd finished, each of them looked at me with tears in their eyes.

"Well, it certainly wasn't a story I was expecting," Trinity said, wiping her nose.

"No." Peggy blew her nose too. "It's certainly heart-breaking and beautiful."

I looked at them both, eyes red, as they reached for a tissue as well. "What do I do?" I questioned.

"I can certainly see why you have the instinct to run. Only makes sense," Peggy said.

"I agree," Trinity answered. "It's not the right thing, though."

"What do you mean?"

Trinity grabbed the piles of books that I'd been looking at and put them back on the shelf. "Well, you ran once. I totally understand why you did. However, now, it's different. I've seen how Connor looks at you, I've seen the way he treats you. I've also seen him when he was with Ella. There is a difference."

"There is?" I looked over at Peggy, who sat there nodding.

"Yes, most definitely. Connor loved Ella, there was no

doubt. However, the way he looks at you can't compare. I can see the difference as well."

"So, running isn't what you need to do. It's easier, most definitely. I think you need to speak with both Connor and Ella's parents. However, if we know Connor, which we do, he has probably already voiced his opinion to them."

"And he is probably on a panic-stricken search through town looking for you right now."

"You think so?" I questioned.

Both ladies nodded. "We know so."

I sat there for a moment thinking about what they had said. The more I thought about talking to Connor, the more worried I became. The more running was the exact thing I needed and wanted to do. "I don't know, Florida looked really nice," I replied.

"Of course, it does. However, will it look nice in ten years, when you return to Willow Valley for a birthday or the holidays and find Connor married to someone else?" Trinity asked.

The thought they'd just projected made me feel ill. I shook my head and sniffled. "No."

"Will it look nice when, once again, regret hits you at seeing him in the streets with his son or daughter? The son or daughter that could have been yours?"

"No."

"Then I think you have your answer."

Trinity and Peggy had gotten me a cup of tea, and I sat with them both until I calmed down. I felt lighter as I left the store. The streets were a little busier tonight, since Christmas was around the corner. I was just about to climb into my truck, still undecided whether I should go home or stay in town for a bit, when I caught sight of both Bill and Paula walking toward me. Anger flooded me along with all the hurt from this morning.

I needed to deal with all the things I was feeling, and I knew I wouldn't be able to do that at home. I sat there for a moment and then fired up the engine and pulled away from the curb. I turned the truck onto the road leading out of Willow Valley. It was already dark, and I knew it was only a few hours to Gram's and Gramp's place. I headed there. I had paperwork to sign to close on the house, and I had to get the few things that I'd left behind. I couldn't go home. I needed space.

3 Days Later

A knock at the door pulled me away from the last box I was packing. Hoping it was the company to pick up all the furniture, I finished wrapping Gram's teapot and headed to the door. It was a complete déjà vu moment as I pulled the door open to see my brother standing there.

"Gabe? What are you doing here?" I asked, shocked to see my brother.

"I came to find you, Cadence."

"Well, you found me." I smiled and stepped to the side to let him into the house.

Gabe looked at me, a frown on his face. "Why did you run away?" he asked, crossing his arms in front of his chest.

"I didn't run away. I came out here to tidy things up, sign the paperwork."

Gabe met my eyes and shook his head. I knew he didn't believe a word I said. He leaned against the wall and shook his head. "You could have done the paperwork through email. I arranged for the realtor to have a company come for the furniture. That way, you didn't need to come out here. So, try to tell me again...the truth this time."

I looked around the room and then back at my brother. "Fine, I needed to get a way for a bit and clear my head. Now, what are you doing back already? I was to pick you up on the twenty-third."

"What do you think I'm doing back? Connor called,

worried sick that you didn't return home. Everyone is worried about you."

"Everyone needs to relax," I replied, moving my way back into the kitchen with Gabe following closely behind.

"Cadence, people are worried. They care about you. Hell, I rushed across the country to get home when Connor called me. The entire flight home I imagined some horrible things. Like it or not, people care about you."

"Yep, sure everyone is worried about me. If that is the truth, they wouldn't have made me feel the way they did. As for you, I'm sorry I made you worry, and I'm sorry you rushed across the country. Does that mean they will cut your leave short?" I questioned, reaching for my favourite teacup to wrap.

"Don't worry about my leave, Cadence. That isn't what matters."

"Sure it matters," I said.

"No, it doesn't. But you do. So do all those who love you. Those who are worried about you."

I could feel my muscles tightening in my back as my brother stood there waiting for me to say something. "You know, Gabe, I've heard that everyone cares about me before. If that were true, then Connor wouldn't have acted how he did. Don't pretend like you don't understand because I'm sure he already told you everything."

"Yes, he told me. Now, fine, you came out here to clear

your head, but where were you going after you were finished here?"

"Where was I going? What do you mean?"

"Exactly what I asked."

"Oh my god, Gabe. I was returning to the damn farm to look after everything, and to pick you up. Where did you think I was going?"

Gabe pulled out a chair and sat down. "You act all shocked to hear the question. It's not unlike you to run."

I finished wrapping the teacup and then closed the lid on the box, picked it up and shoved it out on the back porch. Then I came back into the kitchen and pulled the last two sodas from the fridge and handed one to Gabe.

"Well, I'm not running. I'm cleaning up the last few things I want, getting rid of the furniture and appliances and will be on my way back."

Gabe looked around the room at the few things that remained, then glanced at my small bag that sat beside the back door. "When were you planning on heading back?"

"As soon as this company is here to take the furniture away."

He nodded and took another drink of his soda, then met my eyes. He said nothing, just studied me.

"Just ask what you want to know," I grumbled.

"What do I want to know?" he asked, holding out his hands in innocence.

"You want to know when I'm going to see Connor or

speak to him?" I said, running my finger around the edge of the pop can. "Or perhaps, you were wondering why I didn't call and tell him where I was and when I was returning."

Gabe shook his head. "No…"

"Gabe, don't deny it. I know that is what you were wondering and the answer, for your curiosity, is I don't know."

He was about to say something when someone knocked on the front door. I got up from the table and went and opened it, welcoming the guys who were picking up the furniture, and went back into the kitchen to where my brother still sat.

The second I sat back down, Gabe looked over at me and shook his head. "Cadence, please."

"Gabe, please, enough. I'm going home. Whatever happens between Connor and I is between us. Now, let's get this stuff out of here and get on the road."

Cadence

I sat in the living room, a cup of tea at my side and a roaring fire going in the fireplace. Gabe and I had been back in Willow Valley for almost four days. I pulled my shawl tighter around my shoulders and turned on the tree that sat in the corner. It was Christmas Eve. Gabe had gone into town to pick up some last-minute things for the holidays while I stayed and made dinner.

I'd just shoved a chicken into the oven and had put another log on the fire. It was getting late. I wandered over to the window and looked outside at the snow that was peacefully falling. I pulled the blinds, hoping to keep the heat in this old farmhouse, and turned on the TV, curling up under the blanket on the couch.

Over the past couple of days, I'd picked up the phone to call Connor twice, but both times, I'd hung up. I needed to go over exactly what I'd tell him in my mind before speaking to him. I was about to pick up the phone again while Gabe was gone, but I heard a noise outside.

I got up off the couch and looked out. Nothing was out of the ordinary, except for a light on in the barn. I frowned. It was dark now, and Gabe's truck wasn't outside. I'd only checked an hour ago, and the light hadn't been on. I knew all the farmhands should be gone by now unless they'd forgotten something.

Dropping my shawl on the couch, I slid my boots on and stepped outside. I didn't want to go outside, but I also didn't want that light on all night. I grabbed my coat off the hook and pulled the door open.

I made my way over toward the barn, careful not to slip, and pulled the door open. I frowned at what I found. Connor's truck was inside the barn. Attached to it was his small horse trailer.

"What on earth?" I exclaimed, stepping around the truck until I could see Connor over by Ember's old stall.

He came walking out of the stable, a serious look on his face.

"Gabe's not here," I barked.

"I'm not here to see Gabe. I'm here to see you, and I'm glad you're here," he said, closing the door and latching it shut.

I did my best to fight back the tears I could feel getting ready to fall. I crossed my arms in front of me. No matter how much time had passed, no matter how hurt or how angry I was, I still wanted to run into his arms. I just couldn't allow myself to. I needed him to know he couldn't do this to me. He couldn't just allow Bill and Paula to walk over him, or me.

"What's going on?" I asked, my tone firm.

Connor looked at the floor. "Well, I thought I'd bring over your Christmas gift," he said, stepping back and gesturing for me to come over and see.

I looked around, let out a breath, and took a step over toward him, glancing inside Ember's stable. Cinnamon stood inside the stall, a large red bow on the horse. "What is Cinnamon doing here?"

"Well, see, Cinnamon, he really likes you. So, I'd planned on giving him to you a few weeks ago but knew you wouldn't accept him. Now, since he is a Christmas gift, it would be rude for you to give him back."

I fought against the welling tears. This was way too hard. I wasn't ready to love another horse, and I wasn't ready to love Connor the way I did either. The love I had for him ran deeper than I thought, and it wasn't until he stood in front of me that I'd realized it.

"I know what you're going to say," Connor said, stepping toward me.

"What is that?" I questioned, taking a step back.

"That you aren't ready to love another horse," he said, still coming closer.

I bit the inside of my cheek, trying to put my focus on the pain I was inflicting on myself so I didn't cry and rush into his arms. "It's the truth," I said, my voice cracking, taking another step back.

"Well, Cadence, the truth is..." He stepped toward me again. "I wasn't ready to fall in love again either. Yet, here I am, in love with a woman I never thought I'd get a chance with. But the good thing is that she makes it so easy to love her. Just like Cinnamon here. He makes it easy."

I could feel the burn in my eyes now. There was no hiding it anymore, no fighting these tears because when I blinked, the tears spilled over my eyes, running down my cheeks. "Fuck," I muttered under my breath, rushing to wipe them away.

"I never should have let you leave the other morning," Connor said, stepping closer to me, now placing his hands on my arms. "I should have locked that fucking door. I should have stood up for you, for us. Instead, I fucked up. I know it."

I couldn't back up anymore. I was against the barn door, and Connor stood so close I could feel his breath on my cheek.

"I'm sorry I fucked up," he whispered, his large hand cupping my cheek. "I should have stood up for us," he replied, pressing a kiss to my forehead.

His scent invaded me, the warmth of him comforted me, as I fell against his chest. "Why didn't you?"

"Cadence, that's a question that I will forever try to answer. Why didn't I stand up for us? Why didn't I turn Ella down, and why didn't I just ask you out all those years ago?" He held me tight against him. "I hate myself every time I think of it," he whispered.

Silent tears ran down my cheeks as we stood there in that barn. "Don't hate yourself," I whispered.

"I can't help it. I hated seeing the look in your eyes that morning and knowing it was all because of me and my words. It broke me when you drove away and didn't return that night."

"I needed time, Connor. I needed to think."

"About?"

I slowly let him go. "About us," I said, my voice low.

"What about us?" he asked, taking a step back.

"When I faced her parents that morning, everything became so real, it scared me. I slept with you. Then to see the look on their faces, the look on yours. She was my best friend! They treated me like family, even though I'd pushed her away, all because I was jealous of what she had with you. I was angry. Then to see Olivia standing there, realizing that she was related to Ella, and they had brought her to take you. It was all too much. I just got you, and suddenly I was faced with the threat of losing you. I needed time to search myself, to know if I could handle this relationship, however it turned out. I needed time to forgive myself for all the hate I had for her, because I hated her. Hated her, because of you."

Connor nodded, then turned around and faced Cinnamon. He reached out and pet the horse and then turned back to face me. "And...what did you come up with?" He stood there looking at me, his eyes full of hope but also full of fear.

I searched inward, hoping and praying I was making the right choice. The choice I knew I wanted in my heart. I thought about what Trinity and Peggy said in the bookstore that day about regret. I didn't want to make the wrong decision and hate myself forever when I ran into him again. I didn't want to regret things for a second time.

"Tell me, please. Tell me if I should go. I will do whatever you ask, and if me leaving is what you want, I'll do it. I won't like it, but I will do it, because I can't go home not knowing...—"

"Don't leave," I blurted out. "Don't leave. Please, stay."

I saw the tears in his eyes as he stepped forward and cupped my cheeks with his large hands. "Thank God. Cadence, I love you," he whispered before meeting my lips in a deep, slow, telling kiss.

Emotion flooded me as his lips danced over mine. He loved me. He truly loved me.

Cadence

Christmas Morning

"Oh god...Connor...that was..." I rolled onto my back, breathless, my body covered in a sheen of sweat.

"Now that is what I call great Christmas morning sex," he said, placing his hand behind his head while pulling me in for a kiss.

I could feel my cheeks heat at his words. "It really was," I said shyly.

After we made up, we made our way up to the house where, together, we worked together to get dinner finished and Gabe returned. We'd spent Christmas Eve together, talking, laughing, and remembering old times. At the end of the night, Gabe insisted I go home with Connor, where the two of us could be alone.

"Perhaps we should make up a little more often," Connor kidded, tucking my hair behind my ears and cupping my cheek.

"I really hope you are kidding."

"Maybe. Now come over here," he said, pulling me closer.

I lay in his arms, my back pressed into his chest as he wrapped his arm tighter around my waist. The comfort of his touch, his hold, bringing me right back to how things were that morning. I felt his lips on the side of my neck as he kissed me.

"Merry Christmas," he whispered, his breath tickling my ear.

"Merry Christmas." I kissed his lips just as we heard a bang downstairs in the kitchen.

I jumped against him. "I really hope that isn't Bill and Paula breaking into your home to have words again?" I asked, fearing that it may be them.

Connor chuckled as he kissed the side of my neck. "It's not them. I talked with them both. It won't happen again. I guess Paula has been struggling, but they are happy for us. I promise you."

I nodded, kissing the palm of his hand. He rolled me onto my back, holding his weight above me as he lifted himself up on his arm. Looking down into my eyes, he lowered himself and gently kissed me, intense at first, then slowing.

He brushed my hair from my face; he met my lips again, his hand travelling down to my hip, where he adjusted me so my leg was resting on his hip.

"You really like this position?" I questioned.

"Love it," he whispered. "You know what other position I love?"

I shook my head, unsure of what he was going to say.

"Want to find out?" he asked.

I barely nodded my head. The look in his eyes told me I needed to be prepared for what was coming.

He gripped my hip, leaned down and whispered into my ear, "Flip over."

I could feel myself blush as I rolled over onto my stomach. Once in that position, he guided me up onto all fours and pulled me back against him, his large hands on my hips.

"Ready?"

I didn't have a chance to say anything. I could already feel him pressing against me and, with one quick movement, he'd buried himself deep inside of me, filling me full.

"Oh god. Connor...." I panted.

He began moving slowly, deeply, in and out of me, then brought his hand around where his fingers danced over my clit.

"Relax, baby, just enjoy." He breathed hard as he pumped in and out of me, every once in a while, pulling me tightly against him, entering me so deeply it hurt.

"I can barely take it..." I cried as he continued strumming his fingers over that sensitive little nub at a quick pace.

I could feel my release building and him getting larger. I reached back, placing my hands on his thick, muscular thighs and could feel his muscles getting tense.

"Connnnn...eeerrrr," I cried as my release finally hit. My body shook as he pumped into me, quickening his pace.

I felt his body stiffen, his breathing pause as his body jerked as he poured into me.

We both lay in one another's arms, dozing in and out, both satiated from earlier. Another bang downstairs told me that someone was in the house. I blinked, the room coming into focus, and rubbed Connor's forearm.

"Connor." I gently shook him.

"Hmmm?"

"Someone is here," I whispered.

"MERRY CHRISTMAS YOU TOO LOVE BIRDS. NOW GET UP." I knew my brother's voice as his words echoed up the stairs.

"God, Connor, what if he heard us?" I whispered. I could feel my cheeks heating at the thought that my brother heard us in bed together.

Connor chuckled. "Then I guess it serves him right for breaking into another man's house on Christmas morning. Perhaps before we get up we'll take another round? What do you say?" he asked, tickling my side.

"My god, you are bad!" I screamed as I fought him off.

I quickly threw my T-shirt on over my head and slipped into my pajama pants that lay at the end of the bed. I felt Connor's hand on the back of my head, his fingers threading through my hair. He tilted my head back, bent down, and brought his lips to mine. "I may be bad, but you love it."

"I do."

Silence fell between us as we looked into one another's eyes.

"Merry Christmas," Connor said quietly, kissing me again. "Let's make this the first of many. Come, before he climbs those stairs and walks in here. I don't want him to see inside this room, where I take advantage of his little sister." Connor winked.

Connor had dropped me off to go and do a few errands while I walked down toward The Crispy Biscuit. I'd needed to come into town to get desert for tonight, for our New Year's Eve celebration, and Connor had a few things to pick up at the hardware store. I pulled the door open and stepped inside the diner, immediately seeing Trinity and Peggy sitting in their usual spot. Both ladies waved, and I waved back, giving them a smile.

"Cadence, I'm glad you came in early. I was afraid someone was going to spot your box of pumpkin goodies on the back counter, hop over and take them." Brooke giggled, grabbing the box. "Did you need anything else?"

"No, I think that should be good for the three of us." I smiled.

"Oh, are you guys not coming down for fireworks tonight in the park?"

"Not sure. Gabe and Connor have mentioned nothing to me about it. Do you think it will be a big turnout?"

"Not sure," Brooke replied as she sealed up the box and wrapped her signature pink ribbon around it, tying it in a neat little bow on top. "Well, if you do, make sure you stop in. We are taking up a collection for Bessy at the inn, and I know Gabe and Connor will want to drop by."

Suddenly, I felt hands on my arms, and I turned to see Connor standing behind me. "What will I want to know?" he asked, smiling at Brooke and helping himself to a sample of a cookie she had cut up on a tray.

"Hey, Connor." Brooke looked at us. "It's not very well known yet, but Harry passed away last night."

"Oh, dear god," I said, tears welling up in my eyes. I looked up at Connor, who wrapped his arm tightly around my side.

"Bessy is moving out to the Willow Valley Retirement Home, and the inn is going up for sale in the new year. We are trying to take up a collection for her tonight, so we'll announce that just before the fireworks start."

"We'll be here, Brooke," Connor said, taking the box of baked goods from her.

"Looking forward to seeing you tonight. It's going to be a hard one, again," she said softly, smiling at us with tears in her eyes.

Harry and Bessy had been founding residents of the town and someone we'd all known our entire lives. Connor and I were quiet as we drove through town, right by the inn, before we turned on the road that would take us out to our farms.

As he drove, I sat there thinking of the last time I'd seen Harry and Bessy. It had been on another sad occasion when I'd returned for Ella's funeral. They had opened the doors of the inn to me and had taken care of me while I'd stayed. Bessy had even sat with me out on the large front porch talking to me about life and loss. I hoped she would be okay without Harry.

It had been hard for me to return to Willow Valley. It had taken courage to face the things that I'd held onto for years. I'd been afraid of facing all the things I'd lost here. I'd been afraid of having to face my demons.

While I'd been here, and when I ran back to the Midwest to clean out my grandparents' home, I searched within myself for forgiveness. I'd needed that time to let go of all the anger I'd felt toward Ella. I knew for Connor and me to be together, I had to work through not only the anger and jealousy I'd felt but also the guilt. I also knew I needed to let go of the hot coal I'd been holding onto for years. That only by letting it go would I heal.

Now, as I looked out on the snow-covered fields of Willow Valley, I realized I'd made the right choice. As hard as it was to face all the pain of loss, anger, regret, and jealousy, something wonderful had come my way.

GET TWO FREE BOOKS

Sign up for my newsletter and I'll send you two FREE books.

https://geni.us/NLSignupBackMatter

Next in the Willow Valley Series is Zack and Iris's story in Scars on my Heart.

After a devastating loss, I move me and my two boys back to my hometown of Willow Valley. Once I know they are going to be okay, I take a job at the local book store. That's where I meet Zach, a single dad, who just took over the local bed and breakfast.

Find out what happens in this return to hometown, single dad/single mom, friends to lovers, second chance at love romance .

Available Now

Follow S.L. Sterling

Did you know that bookbub has a feature where you can follow me and it will send you an alert when I release a book or put a title on sale? Sign up here and make sure you stay in the loop.

Bookbub:
https://geni.us/SLSterlingBookbub

Website
https://www.authorslsterling.com

Facebook
https://geni.us/SLSterlingFB

Twitter
https://geni.us/SLSterlingTwitter

Instagram
https://geni.us/SLSterlingInstagram

Tiktok
https://geni.us/slsterlingtiktok

Reader Group

https://geni.us/SapphiresReaderGroup

Goodreads
https://geni.us/SterlingGoodreads

Newsletter
https://geni.us/NLSignupBackMatter

About the Author

USA Today Bestselling Author S.L. Sterling was born and raised in southern Ontario. She now lives in Northern Ontario Canada and is married to her best friend and soul mate and their two dogs.

An avid reader all her life, S.L. Sterling dreamt of becoming an author. She decided to give writing a try after one of her favorite authors launched a course on how to write your novel. This course gave her the push she needed to put pen to paper and her debut novel "It Was Always You" was born.

When S.L. Sterling isn't writing or plotting her next novel she can be found curled up with a cup of coffee, blanket and the newest romance novel from one of her favorite authors.

In her spare time, she enjoys camping, hiking, sunny destinations, spending quality time with family and friends and of course reading.

To be notified of new releases or sales, join S.L. Sterling's private Mailing List.
https://geni.us/NLSignupBackMatter

Get even more of the inside scoop when you join S.L. Sterling's private Facebook group, Sterling's Silver Sapphires: https://geni.us/SapphiresReaderGroup

Other Books by S.L. Sterling

It Was Always You

On A Silent Night

Bad Company

Back to You this Christmas

Fireside Love

Holiday Wishes

Saviour Boy

The Boy Under the Gazebo

The Greatest Gift

Into the Sunset

Letting You Go

The Spencer Brooks Diaries

Our Little Secret

Our Little Surprise

Our Little Wedding

The Malone Brother Series

A Kiss Beneath the Stars

In Your Arms

His to Hold

Finding Forever with You

Vegas MMA

Dagger

Doctors of Eastport General

Doctor Desire

Doctor Right

All I Want for Christmas (Contemporary Romance Holiday Collection)

Willow Valley

Memories of the Past

To Trust my Heart

Letters from the Heart

What Once Was Broken

Scars on my Heart

The Happy Holidates Series

Pop Tarts and Mistletoe

Champagne and Fireworks

Summer Nights and Fireflies

Vancouver Dominators

Inside the Penalty Box

Ten Minute Misconduct